JA

FALL OF THE ARK

THE PROTEUS CHRONICLES

outskirts press

Fall of the Ark
The Proteus Chronicles

v2.0

Outskirts Press, Inc.
http://www.outskirtspress.com

ISBN: 978-1-9772-4329-4

PRINTED IN THE UNITED STATES OF AMERICA

Dedicated
to

Oriole
My Beloved Wife

Other books by Jago Muir

Crud Hall

Kestler's Bane

Libido – The Hunger Season

Libido – Rise of the Ox

Libido – The Shattering

The Death Wall

A Glenby Harvest

Draw near, my child, and sing with me
A song of praise, a hymn of love
In honor and in fealty
To those descended from above.

Remembering, remembering,
On humble knees, with loyal soul,
We pause a moment cherishing
The tale our ancestors have told.

Sir Tropas and his precious few
Eons ago came from the sky.
Their sacred boat fell from the blue,
On snowy peaks its bones still lie.

The ***Proteus*** *was its holy name,*
And Father Tropas was its king.
The Ark from heaven to us came,
And child, its praises now we sing.

—Ballad of the Boat People

1

To stand in the thunderstorm. What would it feel like? To bare yourself to the elements—the thunder cannons, lightning exploding through the heavy, seething, black clouds—night to day in an instant. Upturned face savaged by furious raindrops hurled like bullets from on high, your naked flesh pelted, drenched, and drowned in the onslaught. How would it feel to give yourself over to this violent weather?

The young man sat at his computer console and stared at the images scrolling across the screen. Should someone ask him why this intense preoccupation with ancient weather patterns, his response would be vague. He didn't really know why these archaic pictures of earth weather fascinated him. But they did. When his daily routine permitted, he often dredged up these old files, many corrupted with age, and sat mesmerized, staring at photos of storms and blizzards, phenomena common on ancient earth but nonexistent on ***Proteus***. *What was it like two thousand years ago on planet earth? To walk along the beaches, to breathe the clean air, to gaze at* *distant mountains and valleys? And the snow! The ethereal snow! The delicate flakes drifting down, caressing your face and hair. What did snowflakes feel like?*

Of course he would never know. His world was the ***Proteus***, a gigantic vessel hurtling through space at seven million mph, one percent light speed, as it had continued for over two thousand earth years. Its destination a mystery, known only by the Council of Elders. No, the young man Tropas Bojeon would never set foot on planet earth, now twenty light years distant across the dark reaches of space. Those early ark travelers who had walked the earth were long dead, long forgotten.

Tropas loosened the band across his lap. His work cycle was almost over. Soon he could leave his little cubicle, negotiate his way down the narrow corridor, and board the hovercraft waiting to carry him home after a day's work. He had trained in environmental technology and accepted this position two years earlier on his twenty-first birthday. He was a weather monitor, stationed high up in the zero-gravity central climate control department. For the past two years, he had spent each workday tethered to his chair in front of a computer console. Spread before him were three banks of dials, which he was expected to closely monitor. He was only one of the twenty "weathermen" whose task was to observe and report any abnormality in the ark's climate—temperature, humidity, atmospheric pressure, air purity, and scores of other factors. In the past two years, he could recall only three times he had noticed unusual readouts, and these turned out to be minor fluctuations, not even worth correcting. Some days, his hardest task was simply to stay awake. This job was the very epitome of boredom, and Tropas was sick of it. To pass the time, he had recently begun opening the ancient earth weather files and relishing the photos he discovered.

Unlike earth, the weather on ***Proteus*** was completely predictable. An elaborate tubular structure ran along the ark's central axis, suspended in zero gravity. This weather tube's multiple functions were linked to the ark's agricultural and climate stability. By creating artificial sunlight, plant photosynthesis was maintained and oxygen provided, allowing human and animal life to flourish. The creation of a 24-hour "day and night" cycle meant that citizens could order their lives according to a consistent, steady time structure based on days, weeks, months, and years. The current date was the year 2134 A. R.—Ark Reckoning. The weather tube, lying about fifteen thousand feet above ground level, was constantly shrouded in clouds, which were seeded so as to produce rain. Every two weeks a gentle fifteen-minute shower would fall, moistening the soil, hydrating crops, replenishing ponds and lakes.

Tropas pushed back in his chair and continued staring at the picture of an ancient earth snowstorm. If the supervisor should suddenly appear and catch him gazing at these old earth photos, he might be fired on the spot. But Tropas could not care less. This was his last day at this job. After today he would never again be a "weatherman." He had submitted his resignation almost a month ago.

Every schoolchild knew the history of the ***Proteus***. Launched in earth year 2131, the craft was a desperate attempt to preserve a remnant of humanity. A huge asteroid was on a collision course with earth. It would strike the planet within a century, and all life would perish—a true Extinction Level Event. Humans would go the way of the ancient dinosaurs. The original two thousand brave souls who abandoned earth and made the ark their home would travel into the cosmos in search of a new beginning, a place for humanity to start over. This was the goal of the ark builders—a bold attempt at the survival of the human species.

But dark whisperings could often be heard—whisperings that the asteroid threat had been a false story, fabricated to hide the real truth, a far more sinister truth. The ark's genesis was somehow linked to a virulent disease that emerged and was spreading across the globe as the ***Proteus*** was under construction in earth orbit. The theory was that the ark had been built to allow a few to escape the pandemic, spreading wildly and destroying all earthly human life. To the misery and misfortune of all, this illness somehow sneaked aboard the ***Proteus***, and the plague erupted only a decade or so after its long journey began. The disease wiped out almost the entire ark population. History remembered it as the Great Death. The disease came to be known as Kestler's Syndrome, named for the Austrian physician who first identified the deadly pathogen. It ran its course with almost 90 percent mortality and then quietly disappeared. Out of an original two thousand population, fewer than three hundred ark citizens survived this early disaster.

These events occurred over two millennia ago. The Great Death was today only a footnote in history. Ark population recovered, and currently about twelve thousand citizens called the ***Proteus*** home. The mysterious disease had never reappeared, but some doomsayers speculated that the organism still lay dormant in the DNA of certain folk, ready to reemerge should favorable conditions be met.

Tropas pushed out of his chair and grasped the edges of his cubicle to right himself. It was time to go home. Easing into the corridor, he gripped the side rails and began grappling his way, hand over hand, down the hall. He coasted the final few yards, slipped through the main wall portal and hoisted himself into the hovercraft waiting to take him home down below. He hated drifting around in zero gravity. It always made him a bit nauseous, another reason he despised this job.

2

Tropas strapped in and waited for the others to arrive. The tiny hovercraft accommodated only four passengers. Presently three other weathermen drifted through the portal and edged into the craft. Tropas noticed that old Kramnic's legs and hips trembled as he eased into the seat next to him. *He looks tired and weak, not very healthy. That's what this damned job does to you over time.* Tropas knew that the old man had flown up daily to work at this job for over a decade. *He won't last another year.*

The men settled in and prepared for the 30-minute trip down to the surface ten thousand feet below. Tropas felt the tiny lurch as the craft uncoupled its moorings and moved away from the docking station into zero-grav free fall. They could hear the small bursts and hisses as the directional jets took over and maneuvered the vehicle into its descent trajectory.

Tropas was constantly amazed at the superb technology behind these transporters. A completely autonomous vehicle, a hovercraft was programmed to carry four passengers from point A to point B without any human assistance. Should any mishap arise en route, guidance control would immediately be shifted to manual, and any of the passengers could easily pilot the craft to a safe landing. The men were trained for this, but nothing unusual had ever happened during Tropas' two years service. Hovercraft transportation was safe, comfortable, and reliable.

"I hear you're jumping ship on us." Tropas glanced at the man beside him and smiled.

"That's right, partner. Today was my last."

"What's the matter, Bojeon? Too good to work in weather like the rest of us insects?" Tropas stared at the man sitting opposite him.

"Not in the least, Sturge. I'm just sick of sitting all day tied to a chair and watching dials that never change. I've put in my two years. If I don't walk away, I'll go nuts. Besides, the pay stinks."

"Can't argue that. What are you gonna do now? You got something else lined up?"

"Maybe." He grinned and said no more. One could describe Tropas as young, intelligent, and creative. Ambition often gnawed at him. He had not yet discovered his destiny, but he rebelled at the thought of growing old as a sky worker, a weatherman. He had already interviewed for another job and accepted a position down below. He would start work in a few more days. He smiled at this thought, leaned back in his cushioned chair, and glanced out the small window beside his head.

The hovercraft descended swiftly and smoothly. The men sat in silence. Tropas could see the ground rise up to meet them. As they dropped lower, he saw that the surface was in motion, moving rapidly from left to right. Houses and trees were carried along at a frantic pace. The hovercraft would have to match the ground speed in order to set down safely.

Proteus' artificial gravity was accomplished through the continuous rotation of its pair of giant cylinders, each five miles long and almost twenty miles in circumference. These were enclosed within a massive outer shell and rotated continuously, eternally, clockwise and counter, so as to provide gyroscopic stability to the craft. Each cylinder moved at a rate of 225 mph measured at ground level. Therefore all ark dwellers within the two hundred square miles of interior surface space were able to experience an earth-like gravity that never ceased. Tropas and his family resided in the forward, or Alpha, segment. The aft circle was designated Omega.

Proteus measured twelve miles in overall length, a titanic craft rushing through the cosmos. The central segments were the huge rotating cylinders, sandwiched between twin sections, fore and aft, each a mile in length. The forward half, or "Alpha" section, contained the ark's water supply—almost 30 square miles of surface and a half mile deep. This huge reservoir was capped with a titanium shield, which protected against nucleonic radiation. Behind this ocean of water were vast caverns for the storage of ark essentials. The navigation crew also worked here, as well as the weather monitors. In addition, one of four nuclear reactors, the sources of almost all energy on ***Proteus***, was located here.

This forward section was also home to SAC. Dubbed the "heart and soul" of ark technology, this massive apparatus was capable of producing almost any substance, any material, from pure energy. The huge machine was eons old, but it still functioned well. Called SAC, or Sub-Atomic Constructor, its energy source was the nucleonic radiation constantly bombarding the ark as it hurdled through the cosmos. Flanges and nodules, coated with osmium and attached to the ark's exterior, were constantly energized by cosmic radiation. This energy was channeled into the SAC and converted to matter. Tropas did not fully understand the physics of SAC, but he knew the creation process was a kind of reversal of the Einstein equation. Instead of energy from matter, it was simply the reverse. Massive amounts of energy—and the source of this energy was as infinite as the universe itself—were converted into matter, according to the code fed into the machine. Over ten thousand codes could result in as many different products. Any element on the Periodic Table, as well as almost any other chemical substance—from chalk to candle wax to cork to coffee beans—could be created by SAC.

The creation process was slow, and it released massive amounts of radioactivity as a by-product. SAC personnel did not last long. Workers generally succumbed to cancer within a year. They wore protective garb and were shielded by thick lead barriers, but the danger always lurked close, like a tiny, evil ghost sitting on your shoulder. Working around SAC was considered the second most dangerous job on the ark—another reason Tropas wanted to get clear of the gravity-free Alpha section. Working this close to SAC made him uncomfortable.

He and his companions were bounced and jolted a bit as they descended. The little hovercraft encountered mild turbulence from surface winds pulled along and racing to match rotation speed. The vehicle accelerated to catch the ground beneath it, and then softly settled onto the surface in its designated landing area. Automated arms rose up to grip the underbelly and stabilize the craft as its engines whined down and stopped. The men had felt the pull of gravity slowly creep upon them as they had dropped to within a hundred feet of the surface.

Tropas climbed out onto firm ground and abruptly turned and vomited. This sometimes happened when he felt the pull of gravity after a day spent in weightlessness. It was embarrassing, but he had no control over his weak stomach. He took out his handkerchief and dabbed at his chin. He shook his head, smiled weakly, and turned to his friends, who had exited the hovercraft and were standing around, waiting for him to finish throwing up.

"I'm sorry, guys. Couldn't help it." He awkwardly stuffed his hanky into his trousers and gazed at his three companions. "This is it, I guess. Don't know when I'll meet up with you fellows again. Good luck to all of you."

"Same to you, Trop. If things don't work out, you can always come back and work with us. Company needs good weathermen." Tropas laughed.

"Thanks, Sturge. But I doubt you'll be seeing me anytime soon."

"There are worse jobs than bein' a weatherman," said Kramnic. "It ain't heaven, but it's high." Laughter and handshakes all around. Tropas waved farewell one last time, turned, and began the mile hike to his home.

3

Tropas lived with his mother and younger sister Marla almost two miles from the outer boundary of Murlington, the largest urban center within the ark and home to around eight thousand citizens. The city, touted as the ark's transportation capital, boasted two large factories, each employing over three hundred workers. The larger of the two built and serviced hovercraft. The smaller installation manufactured the popular four-wheeled electric carriages seen throughout the city. Besides these two plants, ***Proteus***' largest, most modern hospital and medical complex was located in downtown Murlington.

On weekends, Tropas regularly hiked into the city to purchase supplies and sundries. He would walk along a narrow footpath, his lightweight shopping cart in tow, pass under the canopy of branches of a small shaded copse, cross a wooden bridge arching over a tiny bubbling stream, and then trudge along another half mile on into town. He relished these weekly visits. He enjoyed them as a relaxing break from his job of boredom in the sky. He would arrive in Murlington in the early afternoon, stroll around the streets, make his purchases, chat with vendors, listen for any latest points of interest, and after two or three hours, start back home as evening descended, lugging his loaded cart behind him.

Today he turned away from his hovercraft companions for the last time and started down the familiar woodland path. Daylight was beginning to ebb in the early evening, but Tropas knew he would arrive home well before dark. He came to the brief canopy of trees and entered the shadows.

As he moved through the shaded forest, he was aware of the silence. Life in general within the space ark was quiet. Other than animal sounds and those of ordinary human activity, very little else existed that would produce noise. One might occasionally hear the soughing of evening breezes as he walked through the meadows, or the gurgling of streams, but few other natural sounds could be detected. Of course there were the soft rumblings of thunder that preceded the biweekly rain showers, but no lightning flashed, and Tropas knew that the "thunder" was artificial, generated by the weather tube for purely aesthetic effect before the rain came down. No, life aboard the ***Proteus*** was very quiet.

But this afternoon's silence here in the forest was odd. No insect sounds; no small, furry creatures scrabbling about high in the branches. No sound or movement at all, other than the soft plodding of Tropas' footsteps as he walked along the path. It was as though nature was holding her breath, all movement held in abeyance, waiting for . . . what? Tropas shivered in the sudden chill and walked faster to reach daylight. *Just nerves*, he thought. But he could not escape the feeling that something wasn't quite right; something dark and ominous seemed to linger in the air.

He shrugged off these thoughts as his home came into view. In the distance he could see sister Marla. She was holding onto a rope stretched horizontally between a sapling and the corner of Old Barney's shack. She seemed to be creeping along the ground slowly, gripping the rope for balance.

Marla was seventeen and unmarried, beautiful, with a lithe, athletic physique. When not helping with housework, she was either roaming the outdoors or holed up in her room studying ark history, a subject she loved. Her mother Gabriella seldom missed an opportunity to broach her favorite theme: her daughter's romantic future—or lack of one. Marla had no boyfriend—and she needed one, in her mother's opinion. She should be thinking about love, marriage, a future home, with husband and children. These were the natural things that should concern a young woman. Marla, however, seemed not to be interested in affairs of the heart. She was a loner, an intellectual, an apt student with a curious mind. This frustrated Gabriella to no end, but Tropas understood his sister well. She had no reason to go running to seek a mate. If her destiny was to find love, then time would take care of it all.

These were his thoughts as he stood watching his sister from a distance. But he was puzzled by the sight before him. Marla seemed to be floating slowly along the ground while grasping the taut rope for balance. What an odd thing!

"Marla!" he yelled. "What the hell are you doing?"

4

As he came closer, Tropas saw that his sister was lifting, though she was clearly very clumsy at it. Her feet hovered only a few inches above the grass, and her legs trembled unsteadily as she moved slowly forward. She gripped the rope firmly lest she lose her balance and take a tumble.

"Can't you see I'm practicing, Brother. Don't distract me. I don't want to fall."

Tropas had seen his sister lift only once or twice when she was very young. She could rise an inch or two off the floor, but she always lost her balance and fell. Consequently, out of fear, she had stopped exercising this ability. It became a phobia with her. Tropas was surprised to see her trying it once again. He stood watching as she inched along, holding firmly to the rope, and finally reaching the tree. Her knees bent as she dropped to the ground and collapsed against the sapling. She gazed up at Tropas and grinned.

"I think I'm improving. Don't you agree?"

"Why are you doing this, Marla? I remember you

telling me many times that you would never again try to lift. Why have you changed your mind?"

"I've practiced every day this past week. Barney stretched this rope for me so I wouldn't fall and hurt myself. It's a lot of fun, Tropas, and I think I'm getting better every time I try it. Here, help me up." He took her hand and pulled her to her feet.

Skimming was a gift that only a few ark travelers were born with. Skimmers could "lift" by leaping forward and gliding for a distance, hovering only a foot or two above the ground, before gravity gently brought them down. Children born with this gift usually took many serious falls before learning to keep their balance. The common thought was that skimming had no practical value. It was just an oddity, and more of a curse than a blessing.

The phenomenon had been recorded for fifteen centuries. It emerged shortly after the Great Death. No one understood exactly how it had evolved, but the theory was that it was a kind of genetic mutation caused by Kestler's Syndrome. Few skimmers were born in any generation. Currently there were 78 among ark population, all male except for five. Marla was one of these five. The youngest was the eight-year-old daughter of a farmer living in the aft Omega cylinder. The other three were elderly women residing in Murlington. These ladies were spinsters, each living alone, and ostracized by neighbors and acquaintances. Skimmers were considered a bit odd, shunned because it was thought that they were bearers of bad luck.

The most notable male skimmer was Thaddur Kline, a philosopher farmer who lived a short distance from Murlington. Kline was by far the strongest of any known skimmer. He could rise up to great heights and glide almost indefinitely. To Thaddur Kline, lifting was the equivalent of flying. He was also Marla's teacher. Each week she traveled out to his little farm for a history lesson.

Skimming was not something that endeared itself to a mother's heart. It was a taboo subject in the Bojeon household. The tacit understanding was that Marla's lifting was not to be mentioned or discussed. Gabriella Bojeon was a 45-year-old widow living with her son and daughter on their modest farm. Her husband had died in a freak accident a decade ago at the "Little Canyon," where he had been employed as a security fence guard. Gabriella was a strong woman and quick to offer her children advice, a habit they sometimes found a trifle annoying.

In truth, skimming had a rich history in Gabriella's family. It reached back several generations. It was a phenomenon she had witnessed up close from her early childhood. Her great-grandfather had been a skimmer. And the gene was passed on to one of his daughters, Gabriella's great-aunt Clarabelle.

The girl learned early that her lifting garnered her the attention she craved. As a child, she became a kind of celebrity. She designed a musical routine, performed while hovering several feet off the floor. At parties and family gatherings, she was always asked to display her skills, and she would gladly comply. While floating in midair, she would whirl and pirouette, her arms waving and head bobbing. She relished the applause that followed. All agreed that her act was charming and "cute." The children especially loved it. But as years passed, skimming fell out of favor in ark society. Clarabelle, now a grown woman, was no longer asked to perform her little routine. She was not a deep thinker and was unable to comprehend why times had changed. She still craved the adulation she had enjoyed as a child. At gatherings, she would still insist on performing her little dancing "act," though guests now found it embarrassing and a bit of a nuisance. Her mind grew weaker as her body aged. As senility began to take her, the family had her confined to a room at Senior Care. But each day Clarabelle would lift and dance. It had become an obsession, the single activity which gave meaning to her life. As her mind faded, she could be seen each day floating around her room and humming to herself. One day she lost her balance, took a fall, and broke her hip, an injury from which she never recovered. Within a month, she was gone. Gabriella had lived close to her aunt during the last years. She witnessed the woman's tragic decline and demise. She still had memories of a frail, old lady hovering in the air, voice quavering, and waving her arms in a pathetic attempt to gain attention. These sad memories affected her deeply. The day Clarabelle was laid to rest, Gabriella had just turned thirteen.

Years later, when Marla was only two years old, Gabriella realized that her daughter had inherited the gene. Her baby girl was able to hold onto the wall and levitate an inch or two off the floor. Marla was a skimmer. Gabriella's initial reaction to this revelation was fear and consternation. Memories of Clarabelle's tragedy flooded back to her. A daughter who was a skimmer was a daughter who carried a terrible disease. She would become a social outcast. Her life would be ruined. No, Gabriella would not allow this to happen! Marla must never practice lifting, and no one must know of the family secret.

For a year it appeared that Gabriella's wish would come true on its own. The little girl's lifting only caused her pain. She was fascinated by her ability to rise off the floor. But she would quickly lose her balance and take a painful fall. She simply could not maintain equilibrium. She would hold onto something and rise, but her legs would turn to rubber, her little feet would slip out from under her as if on ice, and down she would go. Her arms and legs were continually bruised, her noggin carried bumps, and her nose would gush blood if she landed on her face. Her screams always summoned Mother, who dried tears and kissed away pain. After six months Marla stopped lifting. She was tired of getting hurt. She grew afraid of rising off the floor. Also Gabriella day after day warned the child that this was not a good thing, that she must stop doing it. So for over twelve years, Marla had not lifted. She had told her brother Tropas that she would never again try to levitate. Yet at seventeen, here she was, practicing the forbidden act. Her teacher and mentor, Thaddur Kline, had urged her to begin lifting again, not to waste her talent. Gabriella did not try to intervene. The girl was almost grown. She was free to make her own choices. But she feared that Marla's lifting would in time destroy any chances she may have had for a good life.

5

Tropas knew that his mother disapproved of his abandoning the weather job. “Why give it up, Son? It’s a safe, dependable career, and you’re helping to protect the ark. It’s an honorable profession.” Tropas had had this conversation many times over the past month, since he had announced his decision to change careers.

“Mom, you don’t know what it’s like sitting all day in that little box with nothing to do. I’m going crazy from sheer boredom.”

“Well, it’s a good, clean job and you shouldn’t be throwing it away so quickly.”

“I understand, Mom, but I’ve already accepted another position. I’ll be much happier working on the ground.” She said no more, but Tropas knew he was not going to change his mother’s mind.

Gabriella had been standing by the window Friday afternoon when her son arrived. She came out onto the porch to greet him.

“Hello, Son. It’s good to have you home safe. Go wash up and then fetch Barney. We’ll sit down to dinner in about an hour. And Marla, stop that silly lifting. You know you're going to fall and hurt yourself. You look a mess. Please wash your face and fix your hair. Oh, and put on a nice dress. Did you forget we're having a dinner guest this evening?"

Barney Grumb, sometimes called "Old Barney," was gardener, repairman, carpenter, farmhand, or anything else his job required. He pitched in at harvest time and regularly tended all the farm animals. Barney was a large, cheerful man, and even though in his 70's, was still skillful with tools and strong and accurate in his work. Raised on a farm in Omega, he had crossed the Little Canyon into Alpha as a young man. He took odd jobs in Murlington for a few years until he met Joseph, Gabriella's husband. The two men became friends, and Joseph offered him a job. He had worked for the Bojeon family now for over 35 years. Gabriella considered Barney a member of the family. He lived in his little shack adjacent to the main house, but usually he was invited over to sit at meals with the others.

Barney was devoted to the Bojeons, but he had an independent spirit. Often on weekends he would climb into his old electric car and drive into Murlington. He always returned after a few hours empty-handed. Without a word he would quietly resume work on his current project, or he would go into his little house and close the

door behind him. Tropas was puzzled by these mysterious weekend trips into town. He would tease Barney and claim that the old man had a sexy lady friend waiting for him.

"Humph! I'm too damned old for that kind of nonsense," would be Barney's indignant response. In truth, his visits took him to the Murlington zoo. His friend Casper worked there, and Barney enjoyed chatting and helping with the animals for a few hours. He mentioned it to no one, but his most recent trip into town had left him both mystified and disturbed.

One week before Tropas' final departure from weatherman service, Gabriella had gone out to work in her herb garden. The Saturday morning was warm, and by the tenth hour, she collapsed from heat. Tropas and Marla bundled their mother into Barney's electric auto and drove her to Murlington Medical Center. There, young Doctor Brian Strabo took vitals and examined her and soon pronounced her out of danger.

"Just a little heat exhaustion, nothing too serious. Ms. Bojeon, you should go home, stay cool, and get some rest. Stay hydrated and don't exert yourself. By tomorrow you should be back to normal."

"That's a relief," said Gabriella. "Marla, I'll let you go out and pull weeds. I'll stay out of the heat."

"You should give up on that garden," said Marla.

"Poking around in dry ground. It's just a waste of time." Doctor Strabo gazed at Marla and smiled.

"Tending a garden is good exercise," he said. "It's very healthy. What does your mother raise?"

"It's just a small herb garden. Mom likes to potter around and get her hands in the soil."

"Well, take it easy with the weeds," said the doctor. "They always grow back anyway." Gabriella laughed.

"Very true, but I need to get out of the house once in a while." She looked up at Tropas. "We need to get back home. Here, Son, help me down off this table. Thank you so much, doctor." Tropas took her arm and helped her to her feet. "Marla, you still have time to go to your lesson. You'll have to explain to Mr. Kline why you were late this morning."

"Are you a student of Mr. Thaddur Kline?" asked Doctor Strabo.

"Yes. Do you know him?"

"Not personally. I've heard of him though. He's actually quite famous. May I ask what he teaches you?"

"I study ark history with him once a week."

"Well, I'm sure he'll understand why you're tardy today for your lesson." He smiled again and turned to Gabriella. "Ms. Bojeon, please be careful and stay out of the garden for a while. I'm certain you'll be just fine." As they turned to leave, Tropas spoke up.

"Before we go, could you tell me, doctor, are there any

job openings here at the hospital right now? I'm looking for work. I don't have any medical training, but I don't mind sweeping floors or cleaning bathrooms."

"I don't think there's anything available here, Mr. Bojeon, but you might try out at Swarthout Penal Institute. I work out there during the week, and I know they're looking for new people right now. We had three orderlies suddenly quit last week, so the place is in a bind. I'm sure that if you go out and talk with the chief supervisor, Mr. Bradley Conway, he'd put you on right away."

"That's great news! Thank you so much," said Tropas. "I'll go there tomorrow and see what happens." As they moved toward the door, Gabriella turned.

"Doctor Strabo, why don't you come to our home for dinner one day soon? We'd be honored to have you as our guest."

"That's very decent of you, Ms. Bojeon. I don't take a break from work often, but I'd be delighted to join you. I couldn't get free before this Friday evening, though."

"Friday would be perfect," said Gabriella. "And I'm sure Marla could be coaxed into preparing her famous pork loins with parsnips. She is an excellent cook. You'll be impressed."

"And you can join me in celebrating my retirement from weather service," said Tropas. "Friday will be my final day—a day to rejoice."

"So you're a weatherman. A very important job."

"That's what I keep telling him," said Gabriella. "But he won't listen to his mother."

"I'm a weatherman for one more week, but after next Friday I want to earn my hire on the ground."

"Well, speak with Conway out at the Institute. I'm certain he can find something for you."

"Help me out to the car, Tropas. It's time to start home. Doctor Strabo, we'll look for you on Friday. And Marla, you can stay and give the good doctor directions to our home. We'll wait for you."

"Mother, why did you invite Doctor Strabo to dinner?" Tropas kept both his hands on the steering wheel as they drove home. Barney's old el car grumbled and wheezed down the dirt road.

"Wasn't it obvious? Our mother enjoys playing cupid."

"Oh, Mom, I get so tired of you trying to manage my life. Why can't you just leave things alone?"

"One of us has to think about your future, darling. Didn't you notice how the doctor looked at you? He was practically glowing. Nothing wrong with having a young, handsome doctor as a suitor, maybe even a potential husband if you're nice to him."

"*Mother! That's dreadful!* You should be ashamed!"

6

The temptation had been almost irresistible—to embrace her, to feel her warmth, to press his lips on hers. But to do this, to give in to such urgings, would be dishonorable. And Thaddur Kline was an honorable man. He sat alone in his little cabin after she had gone. Today's lesson had been brief. She arrived late, and he had released her early to go look after her ailing mother. But before she left, he had persuaded her to lift. He wanted her to begin developing her gift. It shouldn't be wasted. When she lost her balance and fell into his arms, he held her close and felt her warmth. He breathed in her aroma, so fresh and clean, and this excited him. Thaddur Kline had been alone his entire life, had never dabbled in romance, had never had a relationship. But he was in love with this girl. This truth overwhelmed him, though his logical mind was shouting out a warning. This is wrong. This is dangerous. He could not deny his heart, however. And he sensed that she too had feelings for him. But she was still a child, and he was a grown man in his 30's—nearly old enough to be her father. A love like this would never be acceptable. Society would view it as a corruption. And he would be branded a pervert, a wicked enticer of children. He was already suspect, avoided because he was a skimmer. People considered him strange. But if they knew of his feelings for this young girl, they would be enraged. There would be an outcry. They would seek him out and punish him severely. No, he must never reveal his love for Marla. These were his thoughts as he sat quietly and drank his afternoon tea.

And what about the girl? Did she have feelings for this man? Marla walked on new ground, and she did not quite know the way yet. She had never given her heart away, had never been in love. But she carried a secret deep inside her. She was drawn to him. His strength, his honor and integrity, his intelligent devotion to purpose—these were qualities she revered. Her heart leaped up when he was near. Her whole impulse was to please him. These feelings sometimes confused her, but they ran deep and delighted her. They would not go away.

One might make the case that this teacher Thaddur Kline was nothing more than a father figure to this teenage girl. After all, her real dad had been tragically taken away when she was only seven years old. She had never had a strong male authority in her life as she was growing up. But this theory would prove spurious. Marla remembered her real father. She could never forget the agony and sorrow she suffered when Joseph Bojeon died at

Little Canyon. She had carried him in her heart and soul, would cherish his memory all her days. Marla would never need any older man to lean on, to fill an emotional gap. No, Master Thaddur was much more than a father figure to this young woman.

Wearing fresh, clean shirt and trousers, and sporting a bright red string tie, Barney Grumb stood in the front yard and gazed up the dirt road that led into town. Gabriella had posted him there to greet their guest and point him where to park his vehicle. At five till six Brian Strabo arrived. Barney ushered the Medical Center el carriage into the graveled space beside the small sapling. As he parked the car, the doctor noticed the taut rope running between the tree and Barney's cabin.

"Good evening, sir," he crowed, as he unfolded out of the vehicle. Smartly attired in an expensive blue serge suit and sporting a colorful silk cravat, the doctor stood a moment staring. Cradled under his arm was a bulky flagon of kelberry mead, a gift for the dinner host. Barney noticed the festive pink ribbon tied in a bow around the bottle's neck. Presently he spoke. "May I ask why you have a rope tied to the tree like this?"

"Beg pardon, sir. That's some of the little lady's doin's, one of her play purdies. She holds onto it when she walks. Not sure why."

"Very strange." The doctor stared at the rope a beat

longer. “Oh, forgive me.” He extended his hand. “I’m Brian Strabo. I think I’m expected for dinner.”

“Right, sir. We’ve been lookin’ for you. I’m Barney Grumb, the Bojeon’s caretaker and handyman. Come on inside.” Gabriella stepped out onto the porch.

“Good evening, Doctor Strabo. You’re right on time. Please come inside. Marla’s laying out the table. I hope you brought your appetite.”

“Thank you, Ms. Bojeon . . .”

“Gabriella,” she interjected. “Please call me Gabriella. No reason to be so formal.”

“Of course, *Gabriella*.” He flashed a grin and continued. “And this is for you,” offering her the flagon of mead, holding it ceremoniously with both hands extended. “I thought it might go well with this evening’s meal.”

“Oh, doctor, thank you so much, but it really wasn’t necessary.”

“It was my pleasure.”

“Let’s go inside. I think the others are at the table already.” They entered the dining area, with Barney following a step or two behind.

Gracelyn Threadgill, dressed smartly in her black and white maid’s uniform, stood quietly near the table as the others dined. The Threadgills were the nearest neighbors, and Gabriella had paid Gracey 25 credits to come over and attend the meal. *Just the right touch of class*, the older woman thought.

Mother graced the head of the dining table, the doctor at her right elbow, son and daughter on her left. Marla sat directly opposite Doctor Strabo. Barney preferred sitting apart from the others, two chairs down from the doctor.

"I hear you'll be joining us on Monday," said Strabo, nodding to Tropas.

"Yes, I interviewed with three other applicants. I was lucky enough to land a job. I'll be pushing meal carts up and down aisles. Mr. Conway wanted me to come in and start that afternoon, but I explained that I had one more week to serve as weatherman."

"I begged Tropas not to give up his weather job," said Gabriella. "I'll worry myself sick with him working out there around all those maniacs. That place isn't safe, Son. Everybody says so." The doctor laughed.

"Oh, come now, Gabriella. I beg to disagree. Security is ironclad out at the Institute. All inmates are kept in permanent solitary confinement. They never see or hear any of the orderlies. Tropas will be perfectly safe." He smiled and looked at Marla. "You're not worried about your brother, are you, young lady?" She glanced up shyly, then quickly lowered her eyes and spoke quietly.

"Of course not. Tropas knows how to take care of himself."

"I'll be fine, Mother. Please don't be so dramatic. It's just a job. Doctor, I'm curious. You're out at Swarthout five days a week. What exactly do you do there?" Strabo stared at Tropas a moment, then shifted a bit in his chair and cleared his throat before answering.

"Well, actually not a lot nowadays. I was Doctor Brownlee's assistant until about a month ago. He was the Institute's chief medical officer until he was lured away rather abruptly by Murlington Medical Center. He works in their emergency room now. So I'm more or less alone these days. I oversee the orderlies, but I hang out in my office most of the time, waiting until my services are needed. Fortunately, they rarely are. I prescribe meds for the prisoners and sometimes assist Doctor Snyder on an autopsy, but in truth, I have a lot of time on my hands. It's rather boring." He laughed and looked around at the others. "I'm sorry. This is not good conversation for the dining table. I apologize, Gabriella." He paused and lifted his glass to his lips.

"This is all very interesting," said Tropas, "but who is Doctor Snyder, and why the need for autopsies? That seems strange. And why were three doctors employed at this prison? Are there things I need to know about this place before I start to work?" Strabo tensed subtly. He gave Tropas a quick, cool glance through slitted eyes. *A very perceptive young man*, he thought. He quickly caught himself, relaxed, and smiled.

"Oh dear, I'm afraid I've said too much already. The mead, I suppose." He smiled again, nodded, and made a feeble attempt at being disarming. The others stared at him, and for a moment no one spoke. "Perhaps it's time to change the conversation. Tropas, my boy, you'll learn everything in time. There are things that go on out at Swarthout that I simply cannot talk about right now. All will be explained later."

"Have any of you noticed anything strange about the animals?" Barney broke the moment with his question, and Brian Strabo was grateful. He relaxed and sipped his drink. He also noticed that Marla sat very still and stared at him from across the table.

"What do you mean, Barney?" asked Gabriella.

"Well, I went into town last weekend to visit my buddy Casper. He works at the zoo. While I was there, I noticed that the zoo animals weren't moving."

"What do you mean, Barney?" asked Tropas. "You say they weren't moving?"

"That's right, sir. All the goats and wolves just stood where they were and never moved a muscle or made a sound. It was weird. And Casper weren't able to explain it either. He claimed they'd been acting that way for days. They'd eat and drink a little from time to time, but then they'd seem to freeze in place and just stay that way for hours. People passing by were starting to point and laugh. But Casper, he didn't think it was funny. He knowed something was wrong with them. And Ms. Bojeon, the cows and sheep we got here are starting to do the same. I don't know what's goin' on."

"I haven't seen any birds," said Marla. "You look up at the clouds and the trees, but nothing flies. It's been this way for days. I didn't think much about it until now." Tropas recalled the strange silence and stillness he had felt that afternoon as he passed through the little forest on his way home. Was there a connection?

"So what's happening?" asked Barney. "In my whole life I've never seen anything like this goin' on."

"Something in the air probably," said Strabo. "It'll pass eventually. Nothing to worry about."

"I'm sure the doctor is right," said Gabriella. "Let's not let our imaginations run away with us. Now how about some dessert? Gracey, you may begin dishing up some of Marla's delicious fruit cobbler. And Marla, after dinner, perhaps you would like to show Doctor Strabo around our little farm. I think he might enjoy some fresh air and a nice, brisk after-dinner stroll. Is that all right with you, doctor?"

"Delightful, Gabriella. I would love to see your place, if Marla would like to show me around." Marla squirmed a bit and shot her mother a quick glance, but she smiled and nodded.

"I guess that would be okay, if Doctor Strabo wants to take a walk."

"Brian. Please call me Brian, Marla. No point in being so formal."

Tropas was in his sister's mind. He could see that she had no interest in this man. Gabriella's attempt at matchmaking would come to nothing. The little drama would have to play itself out to its conclusion. Brian Strabo was an aggressor, and possibly not a gentleman. *When he looks at her, he practically drools,* thought Tropas. *I peg him as a lech.* Marla would find out soon enough. But he knew his sister could handle any situation.

"I realize this is trivial," said the doctor, as Gracey placed the dessert dish before him, "but I simply must ask this question. Marla, I noticed a rope stretched from a tree as I arrived. Barney said you walk beside this rope for some reason, but he couldn't explain why. Is this some game you play?" The girl said nothing.

"Marla, tell the doctor what the rope is for," ordered Gabriella. Marla was silent. She sat staring at the dish in front of her. "Don't be rude, Daughter. There's no reason to keep secrets. Doctor, my daughter uses the rope to steady herself when she practices her lifting."

"Lifting? You mean . . . skimming?"

"That's right," said Marla. "My teacher, Master Thaddur, told me that I should practice lifting, that I shouldn't waste the gift. I use the rope so I won't fall." Tropas noticed that Brian Strabo was stunned. He sat shocked, trying to process this new detail.

"You are a *skimmer*?"

"Yes, I am a skimmer." Strabo continued to stare at the girl across the table. Presently, he collected himself and spoke.

"So, you are a skimmer. What a surprise," he simpered. "I had heard of female skimmers, but I knew there were very few. I was told there were two or three living in Murlington, but I've never had the pleasure of meeting one in person. Such a rare gift, to be a female skimmer. And here is one sitting across from me." The man seemed to be babbling from shock. This was Tropas' impression. Abruptly, Strabo glanced up at the wall clock and jumped to his feet. "Oh dear, I see that it's later than I thought. I must be going. I have an urgent engagement in town. Ms. Bojeon, I mean Gabriella, thank you for a lovely evening and a truly delicious meal. You have a beautiful home. Well, goodbye everyone. I must be off." So saying, he strode out quickly, leaving the front door ajar behind him. In a moment, they heard the electric engine engage and then the vehicle racing up the dirt road toward town.

"What do you make of that?" asked Barney. "He couldn't wait to get outta here. Flew out like a bat from a sticker."

"Haven't a clue," answered Tropas. "The man is strange. Something about skimmers that caught his attention." Gabriella looked down at the dish.

"He didn't even taste his dessert!"

"I don't like him," said Marla. "I don't want to see him again. I think he's cruel."

"That's absurd," said Gabriella. "The man is a doctor. He helps people."

"No, Mother. I think he likes to hurt people."

"Well, I'll be working with him every day at the Institute." Tropas rose and moved to the front door. He pulled it shut and returned to the table. "Something strange going on there. I've got some questions that need answering."

"Well, they's something strange goin' on with all these animals," declared Barney, spooning up his cobbler, "and it ain't my imagination."

Hello, Doctor Snyder. This is Brian Strabo. Yes, I know it's after hours, but I have something I knew you'd want to hear right away. I found one! A female skimmer! She's the right age, just a teenager. And she lives on a small farm right outside Murlington. Right under our noses all this time! Did I actually see her lift? Well, no, but both she and her family claim that she can do it, and I have no reason to doubt them. Her name is Marla Bojeon. Her brother is one of the new orderlies, so a transition should be fairly easy. Yes, this is wonderful news for our project. Thank you, sir, and have a nice weekend.

7

The citizens of ***Proteus*** lived in peace—for the most part. An industrious population—generous, helpful, caring; folks lived out their lives in harmony with their neighbors and the environment—generally speaking. All understood that survival was paramount, and cooperation and structure were essentials. So ark life flowed along from day to day smoothly, peacefully, with few bumps and very little conflict—at least this was the usual pattern.

But people are people, regardless of circumstance; to be human is to be imperfect, flawed. Each of the ark's quadrants was governed by a magistrate, who commanded a corps of marshals. These officers circulated among the people to enforce the laws and keep the peace. The crime rate aboard the ***Proteus*** was quite low. Occasional domestic violence, drunken and disorderly brawling, pilfering from shops and open booths when the vendor's back was turned. These petty offenses were rare, and the guilty were summarily punished with fines, public shaming, and incarceration. Each of the four urban centers contained a tribunal where justice was swiftly dispensed. Many culprits found themselves confined to the jail cell for a day or a week or longer.

But there are always a few whose souls are thoroughly corrupt. They are infected with a moral cancer so extreme that they are beyond help or redemption. These are the murderers, rapists, child molesters, and sadistic torturers who move about within a society and commit their monstrous deeds. So it was with the ***Proteus***. Currently, out of the general ark population of twelve thousand, there were 45 men whose crimes were so heinous that they were judged dangerous beyond recovery. In other societies, these creatures would be put to death. However, the Council of Elders long ago had banned capital punishment. No inhabitant of the ark would have his life taken from him, no matter how abominable his crime. No, these 45 wretches had been sentenced to permanent solitary confinement. They would be isolated and forever denied any sort of direct human contact. This punishment had been deemed by the Council as fitting and not at all cruel or unusual. They were to be warehoused at the ark's only prison—Swarthout Penal Institute, right outside Murlington, the ark's largest city.

Tropas sat with three other new employees in a conference room at Swarthout. They had been instructed to report by the seventh hour for early-morning orientation before beginning their first day of work. Doctor Strabo stood before them.

"Good morning, gentlemen. I am Doctor Brian Strabo. Thank you for coming in so early. I won't keep you long. There are certain rules that you must follow, and I want to touch on these and make certain you understand them.

"You four men essentially have only two responsibilities: to feed the pukes and to monitor them constantly. We currently have 45 of these animals locked up in individual isolation cells. They have been sentenced to permanent solitary confinement. For the remainder of their miserable lives, they will never again have any sort of intimate, personal interaction with another human being. They have been removed from society forever. This rule is inviolable and unbreakable. It must be obeyed. They must never see you or any other person in the flesh, and you must never make any attempt to communicate with them in any fashion. If you break this law, you not only will be discharged from service, but you also will have earned yourself two years in prison. I hope I'm making myself very clear on this point. Are there any questions so far?" He paused as a hand went up.

"I have a question, sir."

"And you are Mr. . . . ?"

"Babson, sir. I was curious about these special inmates' living conditions. For instance, how large are their cells?"

"Each man lives in a fifteen-by-thirty foot room, with a small toilet and shower stall at the rear. The cells are actually quite comfortable. There's plenty of space to move around and exercise. Also each cell contains various amenities that make life a bit more pleasant."

"What kind of amenities?"

"Ah, Mr. Babson, you're quite the curious fellow this morning." He smiled and continued. "Each man has in his cell a sophisticated sound system with hundreds of music knobs to choose from. If he is a musician, he may request any musical instrument that pleases him and play to his soul's content. All the cells are soundproof, however, so unfortunately there's no one to appreciate his virtuosity. He may request books simply by scribbling the title on a piece of paper and sending it out with his empty food tray. If the book is available, we send him the audio wafer right away." Tropas raised his hand. "Yes, Mr. Bojeon?"

"Am I correct in assuming that he receives no letters nor has any visitors?"

"That is precisely the case. As far as the world is concerned, the man does not exist any longer." Another hand went up. "Yes sir?"

"Does he ever leave his cell?"

"Once a week he is permitted to go into an adjacent courtyard for one hour. He can breathe free air and look up at the clouds. He may jog around the perimeter or walk or simply sit and do nothing. The enclosure is surrounded by 40-foot sheer walls, so he is still in prison. When he goes outside, we can enter his cell to search or clean or just have a look around." He paused a beat. "We treat these beasts better than they deserve. We feed them and try to make their lives comfortable—for as long as they live.

"Now if there are no more questions, I'll let you get busy serving breakfast. You will push your food carts down the carpeted corridor, stopping at each cell. An orderly will accompany you this first time to monitor and make sure you follow correct protocol. Do your jobs well, gentlemen." He smiled, paused for effect, and glanced around at each of them. "You are dismissed." *So damned full of himself*, thought Tropas. As they rose to exit, "Oh, Mr. Bojeon, one moment please. I'd like to have a word with you."

Other questions were buzzing around Tropas' brain, but he thought it prudent for the time being to keep silent. For instance, what about medical service for these 45 men? If one had a toothache or developed appendicitis, how would the matter be handled? To be attended by a doctor or dentist would certainly violate the total isolation rule. And what if the inmate goes mad and turns suicidal? Prolonged solitary confinement sometimes has this effect on a prisoner. What steps are taken to prevent an inmate from harming himself? Also, what about other prisoners? Are there other convicted felons housed at this institution? No mention was made of them. Where are their cells? Tropas knew that this facility was large. It sprawled out spider-like. He had not had time to explore, but he knew there were many areas, many offices, many closed doors. What else went on at Swarthout Penal Institute? It obviously was more than simply a penitentiary. There was much to learn. But for now, he must deal with Doctor Brian Strabo.

8

"I'm so happy to see you here this morning, Tropas," he gushed as he grasped his hand and pumped it vigorously.

"Why, thank you, doctor. I hope I do a good job." *He is disgusting. I hate having to play this game.*

"Oh, I'm sure you will. You'll fit right in."

"You wanted to speak with me?" Strabo edged closer and placed his hand on the younger man's shoulder. His tone was velvet.

"Tropas, I have a big favor to ask of you. I want you to bring your sister here for a visit. Doctor Snyder is dying to meet her. He's never met a female skimmer, and he would like to chat with Marla." *Something phony about this "request." I don't like this.*

"Doctor, I doubt that Marla would be terribly thrilled at the idea of visiting a prison."

"But Swarthout is much more than a prison, young man. It's a beautiful institution. And Marla would be treated like royalty. I know she would enjoy coming here for a change of scenery. It would do her good, and Dr.

Snyder will be thrilled to meet her."

"I don't know, doctor. I have my doubts." Strabo took his hand away and stepped back.

"Now really, we don't want to disappoint Doctor Snyder, do we?" Tropas sensed a slight edge of irritation. "The doctor carries a lot of weight here. Pleasing him often leads to faster promotions. This will be a wonderful feather in your cap if you bring your lovely sister here. You'll be showing everyone that you're a team player, a member of the Swarthout family. But if you refuse, Doctor Snyder might get the wrong impression. I know he would be terribly disappointed." *I catch the threat. If I don't comply, I might lose my job. But what's this all about? Why is he pissing his pants to get Marla here? Sounds innocent enough, but there's something I'm missing.*

"Okay, Doctor Strabo. I'll see her this weekend when I go home. I'll ask her if she'll come up for a visit. My sister is stubborn, but I'll try to convince her."

"Wonderful! Perhaps she can pay us a visit next week. When you see her, please give her my warmest regards. Now you'd better get along to the kitchen and pick up your food cart. I'm sure the animals are getting hungry."

Tropas knew that his sister would not, under any circumstances, travel to Swarthout Penal Institute for a casual visit. He need not try to talk her into coming. It would be a waste of time. But unless she appeared, they would find some excuse to let him go. Strabo was holding this threat over his head. He needed work, and this job was a plum—good salary, good hours. No, he would play along for a while till he could figure things out. He could put Strabo off for a week or two. He was sure of it.

As he stepped into the hall, a tall, lanky orderly approached him, hand extended.

"Hello, you must be Bojeon, one of the new guys. I'm Trawly Jester. I'm supposed to be your "ghost" this morning—follow you around, look over your shoulder, make sure you're pushing the right buttons, make sure you don't get lost."

"Hello, Trawly. I'm happy to meet you. And I'd really appreciate your help, especially the part about not getting lost. This place is a damned maze."

"Got that right, friend. Let's walk. Straight down this hall and to the right. Kitchen's not far."

Silence. No sound except his boot steps on the polished hardwood floor. Everything spotless, sterile. Bare, white walls, fluorescent lighting overhead, and not a soul to meet, greet, or pass them as they moved down the corridor. The silence was disquieting, like walking among tombstones. Tropas imagined a powerful malevolence watching him, waiting for the right moment to pounce. *Nerves*, he thought.

"Where is everyone, Jester? Feels like this place is understaffed. It's too quiet."

"Yeah, there's not many of us. Gets kinda creepy and lonely at times, especially at night. But you'll get used to it."

"Are you from Murlington?"

"Nah, I was born in Omega D. I grew up in the forest. I used to help my dad chop wood when I was just a kid. We crossed Little Canyon when I was fifteen and moved to the big city. My dad used to be groundskeeper here. A year before he died, he helped me get hired on. I've been here five years now. The work's easy and the pay's good." He paused, and in a whisper, "Bojeon, this place is strange. I get scared sometimes. Things aren't always what they seem. You better keep your eyes and ears open, okay?" Tropas stared at him. He needed answers, but now was not the time for questions.

As they approached the kitchen, Tropas spotted two food carts parked outside the entrance, loaded with breakfast trays and ready to be wheeled around to the isolation cells. Jester stepped to the doorway and turning to Tropas, "Here's our famous kitchen, Bojeon. Come on in and meet the crew."

He peered into the cramped, narrow workspace—a rectangular area with a waist-high counter running down the center. Four staff members were hard at their early morning labor. A short, stocky man had just entered through the back door lugging a heavy plastic bucket. Using both hands, he hoisted it onto the counter and turned to close the rear door behind him. Wiping his hands on his white apron, he reached to switch on a water valve. Tropas noticed that his apron was streaked with red. Beside him worked a younger, taller man, wielding a cleaver. He was busy chopping what Tropas assumed were pieces of meat. Across the counter from them and near the front stood a young woman busy cutting up vegetables. She wore a hair net and her face glistened with perspiration, but Tropas could see that she was gorgeous, with a luscious, svelte figure. The fourth member of the kitchen staff stood over to the right with back to the others. This worker hovered over an enormous cauldron simmering on the stove and was slowly stirring the contents. Tropas was aware of a peculiar aroma drifting from this huge pot and filling the kitchen. He paused at the doorway and glanced over the room.

"This is a small kitchen, Jester, and only four workers to prepare meals for all the inmates. How do they do it?"

"Only four, but they work their magic. You'll see." Then in a loud, cheery voice, "Hey, everybody, I want you to meet one of the new guys. This is Tropas Bojeon. Tropas, meet the team. The fellow in the back with the bloody apron is Jerome. His pal with the wicked cleaver is Hanley. The lovely maiden over there chopping onions is Roselyn. And the cauldron stirrer is Amhearst."

"It's a pleasure to meet all of you," said Tropas.

"The honor is ours," said Amhearst, stepping forward

and curtseying. Tropas swallowed hard to stifle a reaction. He could not catch the gender of this pot stirrer. A masculine frame, but effeminate gestures. A deep, husky feminine voice. Tropas noticed the mascara on the eye lashes and polished nails showing through open-toed sandals, each toenail, a different shade. "Such a pretty boy! Welcome to our glop factory, Tropas Bojeon."

"Amhearst is our resident hermaphrodite," said Jester. "He tends to be a bit outrageous. Pay no attention to him."

"The proper term is 'tranny,' Jester, you imbecile. We don't do the Hermes-Aphrodite thing any longer. It's wonderful being a tranny! Such variety! Trannies go both ways, don't they, Roselyn? Twice the fun." The girl glared and shook her head.

"Amhearst, you're disgusting!"

"Tropas, would you like to learn how we manufacture glop? It's really our specialty, you know."

"Please continue, Amhearst. I'm all ears."

"All the local farmers bring us the tripe and intestines when they slaughter an animal. The Institute pays them well. They come Sunday afternoons and leave their bloody offerings in buckets there near our back door. Jerome collects them early Monday. After brushing the flies away, he washes the guts and passes them to Hanley, the fellow with the cleaver. They're chopped into small pieces, which I saute in hog lard and then boil until

they're nice and tender. Meanwhile, Roselyn is preparing the cornmeal slush and chopping up onions. We mix it all together in this large cauldron, add water, salt, and a few herbs and spices, and set it to simmer for half a day till it reduces down to a nice, thick porridge, and . . . voila! There you have it! Several gallons of GLOP!"

"This is what you serve to the inmates?"

"Three times a day, seven days a week, month after month, year after year. It costs the Institute practically nothing to make, and it's nourishing enough to keep the pukes alive. Maybe once a month, we might toss a piece of fruit on the tray, but glop is always the main course."

"Why do you call it 'glop'?"

"Why, that's the sound it makes when I ladle it into the metal serving bowls. GLOP! GLOP! GLOP! Silly boy, I should think you could have figured that out for yourself."

9

As he pushed his food cart down the long, carpeted corridor, he could hear the persistent "squeak, squeak, squeak," a small but obnoxious noise in the hall's dead silence.

"One of your wheels needs oil." Jester walked beside him, his voice a soft whisper. "You better see to that this morning before Snyder or Strabo comes by and hears it."

"It's just a squeaky wheel," said Tropas. "What's the big deal?"

"When we're this close to the pukes, we don't make noise, no sounds at all. And lower your voice."

"But the inmates can't hear us. All the cells are soundproof."

"Don't argue, boy. It's just the damned principle of the thing. We're supposed to be silent ghosts when we're back here delivering food. And ghosts don't use carts with squeaky wheels. Trust me, if Strabo drifts by and hears it, there'll be hell to pay. Son of a bitch is a damned sadist, and he loves to dish out pain. If he catches one of the orderlies goofing off or making a racket, he'll whip out his cat and give the poor bastard a beating."

"What do you mean, his 'cat'?"

"Strabo carries a white cat-o'-nine-tails tucked in his belt. It's his weapon—a short, stocky handle attached to nine knotted cords. If he hits you with it, you feel it. It leaves scars on your back. This guy is a real piece of work. He lords it over all the 'underlings.' He gets off to hurting people." Tropas was stunned. Marla had been accurate in her judgment of the man. Strabo was a two-faced monster. Mister Wonderful when in polite company, blessed with great social skills. But here at the Institute, five days a week, his true nature surfaces, and he turns into a sadistic brute—assuming Jester was telling the truth. *I guess I'll find out soon enough.* Tropas stopped the cart and turned to Jester.

"Trawly, before we start dishing out breakfast, I need some answers."

"Can't it wait? I may be paranoid, but they might be monitoring us. Right now we just need to be two deaf mutes using our hands to deliver food to the fine folk in the cells."

"No, I need to know some things now. Where are the other prisoners? We have 45 'pukes,' as you and Strabo call them, but no one has mentioned the general population. If Swarthout is the only prison on the ark, then where are the other inmates?"

"Okay, Bojeon, it's time you got brought up to speed

on a few things. If you're gonna be part of the family, then I guess you need to know. To answer your question, there are no other inmates. About a year ago, the authorities made some adjustments. Snyder has some powerful friends on the Council. He got them to agree to a general make-over here. He wants to devote all his time to research. He's some kind of damned bigwig in genetics, and the scuttlebutt going around is that he's been working on some sort of mysterious 'secret project.' He wants to change the public image of this place. Hell, he even wants to rename it 'Swarthout Genetics Research Institute.' I think that's gonna take some time, though. But he did get the Council to agree to get rid of all the inmates except the puke collection."

"What happened to the other prisoners?"

"Damned if they didn't let 'em all go. We had about a hundred. If their sentence was less than two years, they were granted amnesty and sent home. About a dozen long-haulers were transferred over to Murlington lock-up downtown, but all the rest were given a free pass. They couldn't release the pukes because they were labeled 'serious threats to society.' Besides, I think Snyder wanted to keep them here. I'm not sure but the word I get is that he uses some of these poor bastards in his experiments."

"You say he's in genetics? What's this project he's working on?"

"Tropas, I really don't know any more about it. I hear

the rumors from time to time, but I'm in the dark. It's all very secret, and it pays not to ask too many questions. Now we'd better start delivering these trays. After I check you out, I have to go back and fetch my own cart."

"One more item, Trawly. I'm just curious. What happens if one of the pukes comes down with something? Is he allowed to see a doctor or dentist?"

"No way, friend! That would violate the social isolation sentence they're under. These guys are like trapped animals. They will never have any kind of human contact again, not for the rest of their lives."

"So what happens to them? What if one develops a bad toothache?"

"They can request pain meds, but other than that, they just sit and suffer. If they have something fatal, like cancer, they live in agony till they die. Suicide is always an option. That's the code."

"That's inhumane. That's brutal."

"I agree, but these people are monsters. They're getting what they deserve. It's like my uncle Tobias used to say, 'They be shit outta luck.' "

"I can't fathom how anyone deserves this kind of punishment, no matter how horrific their crimes. Eventually they're all going to turn suicidal."

"Several have already gone that route this past year. I'll tell you about a couple weird ones later. Right now you better put these on. I think this is your first stop."

He handed Tropas a pair of white gloves. "Pushing a cart down this carpeted hallway builds up a strong static electric charge. The first time you touch metal, a big, blue spark shocks the hell out of you. Wearing these cloth gloves takes the sting out of it. It's harmless, but it's a damned nuisance." Tropas slipped them on and parked his cart in front of station four.

"Thanks. I believe this is my first customer."

"Right, someone assigned you hall A, the short route. You've got only eight trays to deliver."

Tropas knew that these isolation cells were laid out in a huge square, a quadrangle, each side stretching almost three hundred feet and bearing fifteen cells. A year ago 59 prisoners were housed here. Over time, this number dwindled to the present population of 45, mostly due to suicides. Tropas understood that prisoner suicide was almost encouraged. Nothing was done to prevent it. *These wretches live in misery until their only release is to take their own lives.* This truth bore down on him and made him sick to his stomach. The Swarthout system was a study in human cruelty. These captives were buoyed up with books, music, and physical exercise. But any hope was false. Their only sustenance, a cruel joke—a steady diet of barely palatable livestock gut, day in and day out. Permanent isolation, no human contact. Ad infinitum, ad nauseam. They were pushed to suicide. It was inevitable. But who were these beings? They had been creatures of evil in their past lives. Each had committed unspeakable atrocities. They had forfeited through their vile actions any claim to humanity, to mercy. They deserved this living hell. Perhaps the Swarthout system of punishment was right and true and completely justifiable after all.

He looked at the panel before him. "I think I remember how to do this, Jester. It seems pretty simple." A thin metal plate, designed to slid up and down, covered an opening large enough for a serving tray. Beside it were two buttons, one red, one green. "I push the red button first. This raises the sliding door. Then I place the tray on the roller belt inside. I then push the green button. This does three things. It automatically closes the door; it rolls the tray three feet over to the inmate's side; and it triggers a buzzer in his cell so he knows a meal is being served. Right?"

"You got it, buddy. Perfect. Now let's see you do it."

"Then after giving them an hour to finish eating, I come back around and pick up all the trays. An inmate is supposed to open the panel, set his tray inside, and then slide his door shut. I press the red button first. If my door doesn't slide up, that means the inmate's door is still open. A buzzer goes off to remind him to close it."

"Right. The two sliding doors can't both be open at the same time. That would create a 'communication channel,' something dreadful and forbidden. The puke might see you through the hole. He might say something to you.

You might be tempted to answer him—a capital sin. So what do you do if your door doesn't slide open?"

"I wait ten seconds and push the button again. If it still doesn't open, I make a notation in my little ledger and just move on. At the next mealtime, I skip him. That's his punishment. He misses a meal."

"You're a genius, boy! I'm gonna leave you now and run back to get my cart and start my round. You're on your own."

He knew this job would involve a lot of walking up and down a long hallway behind a pushcart. Meals were served three times daily, and each meal required two journeys—one to deliver the trays and a second trip an hour later to collect the trays and empty bowls. He would be getting his exercise. Then for several hours, either in the morning or afternoon, he was assigned to monitor the inmates. He would sit in front of viewing screens and watch them move about. Each cell contained a small wide-angle camera mounted high on a wall. A monitor was able to observe the entire room. There was no privacy. Swarthout authorities wanted to know what an inmate was up to throughout the day and night—brushing his teeth, masturbating, or hanging himself from his exercise bar.

Tropas parked his empty cart beside the open door and peered into the kitchen. Roselyn was alone and hard at work wiping down the counters. He stood a moment gazing at her. *She is one attractive lady.* He grinned and spoke. “Hey! You work too hard. Take a break and talk to me.” She turned, smiled, and wiped the perspiration from her forehead with the back of her hand.

“Would you like a cup of morning coffee? I think it’s still hot.”

10

"I barely remember my parents, Tropas. They both died when I was two years old. I just have flashes of memory. They were killed in the Omega C nuclear reactor accident about twenty years ago. The radiation leak killed a lot of the workers, and that included my mom and dad. I was raised by my grandfather." She paused to sip her coffee. Tropas sat across from her at the small kitchen corner table. "My friend Helena and I moved to Murlington three years ago and got jobs here at Swarthout. She works down the hall in Doctor Strabo's office."

"Do you ever visit your grandfather?"

"Once in a while. I'm a coward and it scares me having to take the hovercraft across Little Canyon. Grandpa lives alone now. Aunt Bee looks in on him every so often, but mostly he's by himself. Tropas, Grandpa is a skimmer, so his neighbors leave him alone. I don't know why folks think skimmers are evil or bad luck. They're just normal people like you and me." She paused and set her cup down. "You're not a skimmer, are you?" He laughed.

"No, but my sister Marla is. She's not very good at

lifting, but her teacher Thaddur Kline has been encouraging her to practice more. I'm afraid she's gonna fall and break her neck one of these times."

"She's a student of Thaddur Kline? I've heard of him. He's the king of skimmers. A lot of Murlington people talk about him. I think most folks are afraid of him. They say he's weird and evil."

"That's nonsense. I've met the man. He's just an ordinary farmer who prefers living alone. Marla worships him." He paused and pushed his chair back from the table.

"Would you like a refill?"

"No, thanks. The coffee's good, but I'm fine for now." He stared at his empty cup, then looked up at the woman. "Roselyn, You've worked at the Institute awhile. Can you fill me in on what goes on here? Jester mentioned that Doctor Snyder is working on some secret project. Do you know anything about that?" She rose, moved to the counter, and switched off the coffee urn before turning to answer.

"Tropas, I stay in this kitchen mostly and mind my own business. I don't ask questions that are going to turn attention my way. All I know is what I hear through rumors, but I don't know what to make of some of these. They're just too fantastic. I'm real good at keeping my ears open and my mouth shut." She moved back to the table and sat before continuing in low tones. "Helena tells me a lot of stuff. She's cozy with Brian Strabo. She likes to show up at his room with a bottle of rice wine. She'll get him tipsy and pump him with innocent questions. She says he likes to talk when he gets a little high."

"In vino veritas."

"I beg your pardon?"

"It's an expression from an old language. It means "There is truth in wine." In other words, people tend to spill their secrets when they get drunk." She stared at him and grinned.

"How did you get so smart, Mr. IQ?" Tropas laughed.

"I read a lot."

"Anyway, Helena finds out these things and then she comes and whispers in my ear. Also there's Jerome here in the kitchen. I overhear him talking sometimes. He's the hovercraft pilot and picks up on a lot of things that go on."

"The Institute has its own hovercraft?"

"Of course. The landing pad is out in the middle of the isolation cells quadrangle. The doctors like to shuttle back and forth between here and the medical center downtown. Strabo works there on weekends, and I think Snyder goes to pick up medical supplies. Jerome can get them there in less than ten minutes. He overhears a lot and then shares it with us. And then sometimes Amhearst's babbling makes a little sense."

"That's one weird son of a bitch."

"I'm not sure that 'son' is the right choice, but I agree about the 'weird' part. I'll let you in on a little secret, Tropas. Amhearst and Doctor Strabo are lovers. At least that's the general gossip among the staff. They spend the night together often. Amhearst has been seen sneaking out of Strabo's quarters at six in the morning more than once."

"Somehow, this doesn't surprise me," said Tropas.

"None of us can make much sense out of what Amhearst says most of the time. His brain is just too scrambled. But I've heard him babble things about Snyder's laboratory. I think he says something like 'You don't want to go there.' He sings it sometimes while he's stirring the glop pot."

"I haven't met Doctor Snyder, haven't even seen him, in fact."

"He's not very sociable. Stays in his lab most of the time. Now it was Doctor Brownlee who we all liked. He used to come around to the kitchen for coffee. He would laugh and joke with us. I really liked him. I'm sorry he's gone."

"Why did he leave, Roselyn?"

"They say he got a better job offer at the medical center. But I think he and Snyder had some kind of falling out. I think Doctor Brownlee didn't like what was going on in Snyder's lab, so he just quit. That's my opinion."

"This is my first day on the job, Roselyn. I haven't had time to go exploring yet, and this is a damned big place.

Where are the medical labs?"

"They're over on B wing, about a ten-minute walk from here. Snyder has a private lab that he keeps locked all the time. It's strictly off-limits to everyone. I know it has a back door that opens onto a fenced-in yard. That's where all the animal cages are."

"He uses animals in this 'big secret project'?"

"Well, not anymore. Thom Holland let all the animals loose a few weeks ago. That's one of the reasons you were hired."

"Roselyn, you're a very nice girl and I like you. But you're confusing the hell out of me."

"Okay. Let me start over and explain. This little incident happened about three weeks ago. I remember it was right after Doctor Brownlee left us. Thom was just a custodian. One afternoon when he was emptying the trash cans in the main research lab, he did something he shouldn't have. He opened the door to Snyder's private sanctuary. The doctor had forgotten to lock it, and for some reason Thom turned the knob and the door opened. He didn't go into the lab, he just stuck his head in to sneak a peek. But that was a big mistake. We don't know exactly what he saw, but whatever it was shook him up pretty bad. He tried to explain it later, but what he said didn't make much sense. Anyway, while he had his head in the door, Snyder came in and caught him. Thom said the old man went ballistic. He yelled and chased him out of the lab. Then he went straight to Conway and had the boy fired."

"I see. But how does that concern me?"

"Thom had a lot of friends who didn't like to see him go. When they kicked him out, three of his buddies left with him, just out of spite I guess. That left the custodial staff shorthanded. So they hired you and three other applicants."

"Perfect timing."

"There's more to this drama. The day after he was canned, Thom and his chums got some payback. Late that night, they sneaked around back, went into the enclosure, and opened all the cages. Then they chased all the animals out. And there were a lot of them, 30 or 40 different kinds. It was a hateful thing to do, but the boys were mad and wanted some revenge. I don't know what happened to the poor animals. I guess they just wandered off."

Tropas stood and shoved his chair against the table. He said nothing, though his brain and heart were racing. *The animals! Why is this important?*

"Roselyn, do you know if the doctor had done anything to these animals? Had they been used in some sort of experiment?"

"I have no idea, darling, but why so serious?"

"I'm sorry. It's nothing." He set his cup down and glanced up at the wall clock. "I'm afraid I must leave you.

I have a date with my food cart. It's almost time to go around and collect the trays. Before I go, can you tell me one more thing?"

"Of course. What is it?"

"This boy Thom. What did he see in Snyder's lab? You said he was shaken pretty badly. What was it?"

"Tropas, this part scares me. He said there was a narrow cage with bars up to the ceiling. Something was lying on the floor of the cage, something black and hairy. He couldn't tell if it was an animal or what. After a second or so, he said it *moved*! Then a head lifted and eyes stared straight at him. And it growled! That's what got to him. The black thing growled at him. I think that's when Snyder came in. After I heard this part of the story, I couldn't sleep for two nights."

"Sounds like something a kid would make up to scare his friends."

"True, he may have made up that part, but Tropas, it scared the bee-jeebies out of me." He stood a moment gazing at the woman.

"Roselyn, take care of yourself. We should talk later. I have to go now."

"Come up to my room, sweetie, when you have the time. Room 27C. We can talk more in private. I have some rice wine I'll share with you." He smiled.

"It's a date." He turned and walked out to his cart.

11

So Thom and his chums release these lab animals as some kind of malicious practical joke. And a week later all the animals in this region of the ark start acting strange. There has to be a connection. Also, there's a hairy, black monster in Snyder's private lab. This is just too far-fetched. Wasn't there an old story I read once about a Doctor Frankenstein?

Tropas rolled his cart back to the kitchen by the ninth hour. One of the inmates had sent out a slip of paper with his empty bowl. Scribbled on it was a title that Tropas recognized: *The Count of Monte Cristo.* He glanced inside but Roselyn had left. The place was deserted. He remembered he was due to join Jester in the observation room soon, provided he didn't get lost on the way. The two of them would spend the rest of the morning watching prisoners on the monitor screens. *How is this any improvement over staring at weather dials?* He turned and made his way down the hall.

The old man approached him slowly, hobbling along, taking his time. He wore a soiled lab apron and sported a graying Vandyke style beard and moustache. Tropas knew at once that this was the famous Doctor Snyder, though he had never seen him. He stared straight ahead, never glancing at Tropas, as they passed in the hallway. His face was twisted into an odd moronic grin, and he mumbled quietly to himself as he moved along. His mutterings were inarticulate, but Tropas thought he heard him say "medulla," and he was quite sure he heard the word "Kestler." Tropas stood and watched the old doctor as he edged on down the hall. *He should use a cane*, he thought.

"Any action I missed?" He slumped into the padded chair beside Jester and looked up at the row of screens.

"Only George Lee's regular morning jerk off. Right on schedule. Other than that, nothing very exiting so far. They just sit around and do nothing. Or some pace up and down their cells."

"I think I ran into Doctor Snyder coming down the hall a few minutes ago. The guy's really feeble. And he talks to himself."

"That's the old doc all right. After breakfast he likes to go down to the cells and stir around a little. I guess walking clears his mind. He's supposed to be some kind of genius genetics guru, but just between you and me, I don't think the old guy's playing with a full one."

"What's this about a big, black monster he keeps in his

lab? Know anything about that?"

"Ha! That's bullshit, boy. Don't you know it when you smell it? There's nothing in that back lab—unless Snyder has a pet cat. That may be what the kid Thom saw. I think maybe he just made that part up to get attention."

"That's possible," said Tropas, "but nothing surprises me about this place anymore. I've been at Swarthout only three hours, but I'm beginning to feel the rhythm. 'Weird' lives here. It's something you guys work around every day."

"You don't know the half of it, old boy."

"By the way, Jester, who do I give this to?" He brought out the book title slip.

"Drop that by Strabo's office. Give it to Helena. The doctor's in charge of the literature archives. Did you know that we keep over a thousand titles here? Only about a dozen of the pukes are readers, though. It's kind of a waste, if you ask me."

Tropas sat back and concentrated on the monitor screens. Within minutes they all faded to sameness. The men in the cells were little more than inanimate objects. Some paced; two sat on their bunks; one seemed to be asleep at his writing desk against the wall. There was no interest, no energy, no vitality. That was their common denominator. They were trapped and defeated and simply waiting for their lives to end.

"This is depressing, Jester. Why do we have to sit and

watch this all morning? It seems pointless."

"We have to keep tabs on these guys. Sooner or later one's gonna off himself. I've witnessed two suicides in the past four months. We monitors put money on who we think'll bite it next. I've got my eye on number seven here. I think he's good to go any day now." Tropas was jolted into weakness. Suddenly he felt numb all over. This man's lack of feeling was beyond belief. He was completely devoid of any shred of sympathy or compassion. These inmates weren't human beings; they were nothing more than objects of entertainment.

"So you actually wager on who's going to kill himself next?"

"That's right. It gives us something to do so we don't keel over from pure boredom. I saw the last two go. The first guy was one of mine over on C. I forget the bastard's name, but I know he played the flute. One afternoon, he stood up, stuck the pointy mouth end against his chest, and then pitched forward onto the floor. This rammed the flute up into his heart, I guess. He died right there on the spot. I almost shit my pants! I remember he had fifty-to-one odds. Nobody thought he'd do it since he was a damned music lover. He used to play that flute constantly. Benny here had bet ten credits that he wouldn't live till the end of the month. Boy, did he cash in big!"

"You said you witnessed two suicides. Who was the second?"

"Tropas, this guy was truly insane. He had lost it all. We called him Big Anson because he weighed around three hundred pounds. Big fucker! He used to sit on his bed all day and just drool. Anyway, one morning he started smearing his shit all over the walls. He must've saved up his turds. He went around smearing and swirling and making crazy designs, like some kind of deranged Picasso. Then he sat down and picked up some scissors. I watched him stick the sharp end up into a nostril, draw back a fist, and pound as hard as he could. He drove the blade through his nasal cavity and into his brain. Talk about blood gushing everywhere! That just about got to me, brother. It took a pair of orderlies a whole week to clean the cell. You could still smell the stench halfway down the hall."

"These two suicides are the only ones you know about?"

"These are the only ones I actually witnessed. I heard there were four others in the past twelve months, not counting the 'ghost.' "

"The ghost?"

"Yeah, he was an older guy named Slackson. They just found him dead one morning in his bed. We tagged him the ghost because two people claimed they'd seen his head floating in the dark the night before. Crazy, right? But that's just another case of bullshit. Nobody's gonna believe crap like that."

"Who were the two who claimed they saw his head?"

"One was Helena, Strabo's secretary. The other was Hanley, the tall guy you met in the kitchen. Get them to tell you all about their 'ghostly visitations.' How they can dish out that rubbish with a straight face is beyond me. I laughed my ass off when I first heard about it. Slackson conked out in his sleep. No complications. It was just his time to go."

"So that totals up to seven who have died in the past few months. But I understand that a year ago, there were 59 in the isolation cells. I'm confused about the math. If we have 45 now, what happened to the other seven 'pukes'?"

"Yeah, that's a mystery, Tropas. Nobody knows. They just vanished. None of the monitors said they saw anything unusual. One of our missing pukes was a skimmer. We used to watch him float around in his cell. He just vanished one day."

"When you say 'vanished,' you mean . . . "

"Here today, gone tomorrow. None of the screen monitors saw anything out of the ordinary. The cells were just empty the next day."

"Even though all the puke cells have an overhead camera that rolls 24-7?"

"You got it. The guys just weren't there anymore. Go figure it. But I gotta tell ya, there's a rumor goin' around that Snyder used those pukes in some kind of experiment and then afterwards had the 'ghoul squad' bury the corpses in the field out back."

"Did you say 'ghoul squad'?"

"Yeah, that's the name we gave 'em. They're the guys who carry the body out back and bury it. They wait till everyone's asleep—around one or two in the morning—then sneak the dead puke out and dump him in a shallow grave out behind the back fence. At least that's the theory. I don't know if it's true or not."

Tropas said nothing. He sat very still, his thoughts moving in new directions. Could there be any truth at all to these rumors? *Inmates used like lab rats, then disposed of in the dead of night. Something out of a Gothic horror novel. Mystery piled on mystery.*

At half past the eleventh hour he walked into Brian Strabo's outer office. An attractive woman with curly blonde hair sat at her desk, poring over inventory forms. She looked up and smiled.

"Can I help you?"

Helena Gimbal was short and stocky, with a busty upper torso, wide hips, and sturdy legs. Her large, innocent, doe eyes and sensual, cherry lips did little to mask a ravenous libido, which always marched several steps before her. She was a dynamo of energy, scurrying here and there, attending to this job and that, and constantly at Strabo's beck and call. Now her smile widened as she saw the tall, handsome stranger standing before her. Tropas held out the slip of paper.

"I think I'm supposed to give this to you. It's a book request an inmate sent out this morning."

"Tropas, my lad, how are you?" Large, loud voice. The doctor stood in his doorway. "Bring that into my office and let's have a look at it." As Tropas stepped into the inner office, he saw the thing lying on the doctor's desk—the infamous "white cat," a short handle with nine knotted cords attached, a dangerous weapon of pure pain. *He makes no effort to hide it. I think he's proud to carry it.* Strabo seized the boy's hand with both his own and shook it vigorously. "How is your first day on the job turning out so far?"

"It's going fine, sir. It's keeping me busy. I brought this book request I got this morning from one of the inmates. Someone said I was supposed to bring it to you." Strabo took the paper and read the title scribbled on it as he moved around to his chair and sat at his desk.

"*The Count of Monte Cristo*. This is a very popular book among the pukes. They love to read about a prisoner who escapes from an escape-proof penitentiary. Raises their spirits, gives them a glimmer of hope. Are you familiar with the story?"

"Yes, I've read the book. The man's name is Dantes. He escapes from the Chateau d'If and goes on to find a fabulous treasure."

"Yes, yes, well the pukes enjoy it. I'll look in the archives to see if it's available. I'll have Helena leave the audio wafer on your food cart before this evening's feeding."

"Thank you, sir. It's almost time for the noon meal. I'd better get back to the kitchen."

"Before you go, Tropas, let me remind you to bring your sister here next week. I've mentioned her to Dr. Snyder, and he's very excited to meet her. We'll expect her here on Monday. Is that clear?" *What's clear is that he's giving me an order. It isn't a choice, it's a command.*

"I'll do my best, Dr. Strabo. Like I told you before, Marla is a very stubborn girl."

"Well, she simply must come here, Tropas. We're depending on it. Dr. Snyder has declared her an invaluable asset to his project. He needs her input to complete his work. Please don't disappoint us. Now run along and feed the animals." Helena Gimbal stared at him with hungry eyes as he hurried past her desk and disappeared down the hall.

12

After delivering glop trays, he joined Jester in the cafeteria for a bite of lunch. He remained there till it was time to make his second run and collect the empties. Afterwards, his mind turned to Roselyn, room 27C, and rice wine. It might be stimulating to spend a few afternoon hours with a beautiful woman in private quarters. But after a beat he dismissed the thought. This first day at a new job had begun early, and he was tired. He needed to go to his own quarters and catch an afternoon nap. Besides, he knew he had no business jumping into a workplace romance with a new colleague, no matter how tempting the prospect might be—at least not on the first day at work. It just wasn't prudent.

He woke up refreshed shortly before the sixth hour and made his way to the waiting food cart parked outside the kitchen. As promised, he spotted the book wafer, a small, coin-sized, white plastic disk, lying on the top tray. He would send it in to the inmate, who would insert it into the audio slot in his cell. And, like magic, an oral reading of *The Count of Monte Cristo*, chapter one, would begin. The man could pause it with the push of a button and return to it later if he chose—one of the "amenities" the pukes could turn to for relief from boredom.

At a quarter past six, he returned his empty cart to its usual spot beside the kitchen door. He had 45 minutes to kill before making his final evening run. The kitchen crew had finished their work for the day and were lounging around, chatting and relaxing. Amhearst still stood in his place before the stove, waving his wooden spoon back and forth and humming to himself, a maestro conducting his invisible orchestra. As he stood at the doorway, Tropas considered that now might be a good time to ask about the incident Jester had mentioned earlier that morning—Hanley's weird encounter with a mysterious "ghost." Something about this piqued his curiosity.

As he gazed at these kitchen workers, a stark realization burst upon him. Each of these four was as much a prisoner in his own fashion as any of the pukes in isolation cells. Their job was to feed the inmates. And the process of preparing this disgusting food they called glop had to continue non-stop, day after day, month after month, on and on, forever—or at least for as long as there were hungry criminal mouths to feed. They were required to labor long and hard every day, with few breaks. How did they do this without going insane? Were there other kitchen crews to come in, take over, and share the labor? Tropas did not know.

"Come in and join us, stranger." Jerome had spotted him standing in the doorway.

"Sit down and give your weary bones a rest." Hanley had shifted a welcoming chair around for him. Tropas grinned and eased his large frame onto the seat. He was surprised at how weary he had suddenly become. Pushing food carts up and down aisles all day had taken its toll.

"Here you go. Last of the coffee." Roselyn set the cup before him.

"Thanks, you're a jewel," as he raised the cup and sipped the tepid liquid. After a moment he looked up at Hanley, leaning against the vegetable counter. "I'd like to ask you a question, if you don't mind."

"No problem, comrade. What's on your string?"

"What can you tell me about your 'ghost visit'? That green floating head you saw a few weeks ago." This prompted an instant reaction from Amhearst. He launched into song.

Floating head, floating head,
Come and see my floating head.
Giddyap, giddyap, giddyap, my-y-y
Green floating head.

He belted out these lyrics as he pranced up and down the aisle, slapping himself on the rump as if urging his pony to run faster.

"Amhearst!" Jerome shouted. "Cut the crap and sit down!" The horse ride abruptly ceased, and Amhearst took his accustomed place at the stove. He picked up his long wooden spoon and began stirring the contents of the glop cauldron, though it was mostly empty and cool, the burner having been switched off long ago. *This creature is truly insane*, thought Tropas.

"I don't talk much about that." Hanley shook his head and looked down at his cup. "People still laugh at me if I mention it."

"I'm not laughing," said Tropas. "I think you and the woman really saw something that night. Can you describe what happened?"

"Something woke me up, it must have been about one o' clock. I opened my eyes and saw this greenish globe floating over my bed, maybe two feet from my face. It just hovered there, glowing and pulsating. There was a face staring at me, some old bald-headed man with a gray beard and moustache. There was no sound, just that weird face looking right at me. I yelped and jerked away and fell off the bed. I must have hit my head on the floor. I got a cut on my right jaw. When I looked up, the thing was gone and I never saw it again."

"Helena saw the same thing," said Roselyn. "She described the green pulsating globe and the same face staring at her when she woke up. She said it happened sometime after midnight. She screamed and screamed and people came running and pounded on her door. But afterwards everybody said she just had a bad dream, a nightmare. Nothing to get excited about."

"The next day," said Hanley, "I told a buddy about the face, and he said it sounded like Eric Slackson, an inmate they'd found dead in his cell that morning. The dude was lying on his bunk, eyes wide open, staring up at the ceiling. He showed me Slackson's picture, and it was the same guy, an old bald-headed bastard with a gray beard."

"How long had Slackson been in isolation?" asked Tropas.

"He was one of the older pukes. He'd been here in solitary confinement almost eight years. In fact, I think he held the longevity record. Slackson was a serial killer. He'd slashed the throats of fifteen teenagers before they caught him and sent him here. He was a real bundle of joy." Tropas said nothing. He sat for a moment staring at his empty coffee cup. Presently he looked up and glanced around at all of them.

"I have a theory about this, but it can't be proven." Silence all around.

"Go ahead. We're listening," said Hanley.

"Are you familiar with the phenomenon called 'astral projection'?"

"*Asshole protection! asshole protection!*" quacked Amhearst. Jerome glared at him and he grew silent, slowly stirring the empty glop cauldron.

"Please enlighten us," said Roselyn.

"Astral projection, also called 'out-of-body experience,' was a phenomenon dating back to ancient earth. It was believed that some people, while in a deep sleep, could leave their physical bodies and drift around. Their consciousness or soul or spirit could separate from the physical form and float around the local vicinity to observe and listen. The consciousness was attached to the sleeping body by some kind of cord, so it couldn't go far and could eventually find its way back to rejoin the sleeper."

"So you're saying that what Helena and I saw was Slackson's 'consciousness' that had separated from his body back in his cell?"

"Sounds crazy, I know," said Tropas. "But there's a kind of bizarre logic to it. You said that Slackson had been in complete solitary confinement for almost eight years? I think the old codger was desperate for human contact. Maybe he knew his life was nearing its end, and he was starving for the sight of another human being, a real person in the flesh. This was the only way he could pull it off. Maybe what you saw was his astral projection. He wasn't there to hurt you. You said he vanished when he sensed your emotional response."

"If you call pissing your pajamas and falling out of bed an 'emotional response,' then I suppose you're right."

"Hell, he probably just wanted to be your friend," said Jerome.

"If floating around your bedroom after midnight and scaring the hell out of you was his idea of courting friendship, then I think the fool needed to work on his social skills."

"Tropas might be on to something," said Roselyn. "Hanley and Helena both saw the exact same image at about the same time at night—the face of an inmate neither had ever seen before, an older inmate close to death. I think the evidence is very compelling."

"I agree, it's an interesting theory," said Hanley. "Real food for thought. But we'll never know the truth. Thanks for enlightening us, buddy." Tropas rose and moved to the door.

"Goodnight, friends. I have one more cart run to make and then I'm heading for bed. I've had a long day."

"Sleep well," said Jerome.

13

Early Tuesday morning Barney stood at the Bojeon front door waiting for someone to answer his knock. Presently, Gabriella appeared. “Good morning, Barney. You look perplexed. Is anything the matter?”

“I’m sorry, Ms. Bojeon. Some really bad news. All our animals is dead. The two milk cows, the sheep and pigs, and all our chickens. I found ‘em all dead this morning. I’m afraid we’re gonna be short on food within a month.”

“This is terrible, Barney. What happened to the poor creatures? Did hungry wolves get at them?”

“No ma’am. I figure it was some kind of disease. They’ve all been still as statues for the last day or so—like what we talked about at dinner Friday when the doctor was here. The critters finally just keeled over one by one and died.”

“Well, we mustn’t despair. We’ll deal with misery when it falls our lot. But in the meantime, we must stay hopeful. We’ll get by somehow. What will you do with our poor animals?”

“I’ll drag ‘em out to the pasture and bury ‘em this

afternoon, ma'am. But this morning I'd like to go into Murlington and visit with my friend Casper, see how him and his zoo animals are gettin' on."

He walked down a deserted street. No citizens wandering about, no movement, no usual clamor of a bustling metropolis. Murlington had become a dead city. Businesses were closed, their doors and windows shut tight. Nothing but a bizarre silence and stillness. Abandoned el carriages could be seen here and there, parked up and down the avenue, but their drivers had vanished.

Barney had hiked to the city and stumbled into this dreamlike scenario. He walked along in utter amazement. *Where are the people? What is going on here?* As he paced along the sidewalk, he detected movement in an alleyway across the street. Some black thing was lurking behind a trash bin—this was how it struck him—but it had quickly disappeared. Had he imagined it? He couldn't be certain.

Arriving at the municipal zoo, he spotted Casper stirring around inside his small office. Making for the door, he glanced over the visitor fence for any sign of animals, but there were none to be seen.

"Hello, Barney. What are you doing here?" He left off rummaging in his desk drawer and stared at his friend.

"I just dropped by for a visit. You're the first soul I've run into since I got to town. Where is everybody, Casper?

What's goin' on? And where are your animals?"

"The animals are all dead, Barney. My three little goats were the last ones left. They had stood in place for two days, not moving a muscle. And then yesterday they just fell over dead, one by one. I felt like crying."

"That's too bad. But where are all the people? It's like a ghost town out there."

"Barney, everybody's scared. I figure most folks have locked themselves in their homes and are afraid to go outside. There's a disease going around, and people are dying in droves. The Medical Center Hospital is overflowing from what I hear. Sick folks are dying in the hallways and the waiting rooms. A lot of us are getting away, heading out of town. I hear some of the medical staff have already quit and left the city. That's what I'm doing right now. I stopped by here to pick up a few things, but I've got my travel bag packed, and as soon as I can find an el-car with some charge left in the cylinders, I'm outta this city. I'm gonna drive down to my cousin's farm close to Little Canyon. It's ten miles from here and as far as you can get from Murlington without crossing over into Omega. I'd invite you to come along with me, but I know you've got your own people to take care of. If I was you, I'd hurry on back home and get the family ready to move someplace far away from here. Your farm is just too close to this city, and I think the evil is spreading. Be careful. People I've talked to claim they've seen some big, black, ape-like critters stalking around, digging in garbage cans, looking for food. I don't know if this is true or just rumors, but I'd be careful. These are strange times we're livin' in, Barney, *strange* times."

Tropas had breakfast in the kitchen after his Tuesday morning meal run. "We cook our own meals here," said Roselyn. "Everything in the cafeteria tastes like cardboard."

"Very true," said Tropas. "I noticed that yesterday. You guys sure know your way around a kitchen. I have to ask you, are you the only group that comes in here to do this work? Or is there another kitchen crew to share the duty and give you a break now and then?"

"Nope, there's no B-team. It's just us," said Hanley.

"And we show up early every morning at the sixth hour to start our day," said Roselyn.

"We don't complain," said Jerome. "This work's not that hard, and we have our glop system down to a fine art."

"They give us a day off once a month," said Roselyn, "as long as we whip up an extra batch a day ahead of time. A couple of workers can just come in here, dish up the glop, and put the bowls on the food carts, easy as can be."

"I see," said Tropas. "I clearly am working with true artists. I admire your stamina."

"Have any of you heard the weird news?" asked Hanley.

"One of the orderlies went into Murlington yesterday to visit his folks. He came back this morning spouting off some really strange stuff. He claims an epidemic has broken out in the city and a lot of people are dying. He says the streets are empty because folks are scared to go outside. Hundreds are panicking and leaving town."

"Sounds like exaggerated bullshit to me," said Jerome. "Any time some sickness breaks out, there's always a few prophets of doom who go around crying 'The end is near!' or 'It's the end of the ark!' "

"I also heard that animals are dying everywhere," said Hanley. "Some are saying that without animals, the atmosphere will get screwed up—something about the oxygen and carbon dioxide balance. This might cause crops and plant life to start dying. It sounds real serious."

"It's freakin' funny, if you ask me," said Jerome. "After the emergency passes and life gets back to normal, everybody sees that these dire predictions of impending doom were pure horse hockey. I wouldn't pay them any mind."

14

Shortly after the ninth hour, Tropas returned his cart to the kitchen, completing the morning ritual. He now was free till half past eleven. He had the morning off, with nothing to do. He stood a moment in the doorway watching his four friends hard at their accustomed labor. *They seem happy preparing the next batch of glop. It's as though they were born for this job.* Roselyn caught his eye, smiled, and nodded toward the coffee urn, as if to say "Help yourself." He moved to the counter, fetched a cup to pour, and then took a chair in the corner to sip the fresh brew. He liked these four; he was comfortable in their presence. Though only into his second day at Swarthout, this kitchen had already become his favorite place to hang out. These four had accepted him in friendship and, in a real sense, had "adopted" him as one of their own. He relaxed, drank his coffee, and watched them work.

After a time, Hanley completed his chopping and laid his cleaver aside. He came to the corner table and stood a moment staring at Tropas, arms akimbo.

“You realize you’re the current celebrity here at this institute, don’t you?”

“What?”

“Word gets around. All the little people are talking about you.”

“Really? What are they saying?”

“That you have a sister named Marla, that she’s a skimmer, and that Snyder and Strabo are aching for you to bring her here for a visit.”

“Although no one knows why exactly,” said Jerome, who had come over to stand by his friend.

“This is all true,” said Tropas. “Strabo claims that Snyder needs her so that he can complete his mysterious ‘secret project.’ But I don’t like the sound of it. And besides, Marla isn’t about to come anywhere near here.”

“Don’t be too sure, pal.” Hanley had spoken. “Snyder has some powerful friends on the Council. He usually gets what he wants.” Roselyn came to the table and sat.

“We’re all curious about your family, Tropas. I understand that you and your sister live with your mom on a little farm a few miles out of Murlington.”

“That’s right. We have a handyman named Barney who lives with us. He’s part of the family. But it’s just the four of us.”

“What about your dad?” asked Jerome. “Is he still living?”

“No, Dad was killed ten years ago in an accident at

Little Canyon. He worked there as a security fence guard. The local shuttlecraft pilot and his wife and kid lived in a little bungalow near the fence. The boy had a pet dog, a puppy, and it seems that the animal slipped through the fence one afternoon and began chasing after a piece of scrap paper blowing on the ground. Dad saw that the little dog was running toward the canyon edge, and he made a foolish decision. He started chasing after him. He wanted to save the puppy for the little boy. He was halfway across the Death Zone when the wind caught him. He was lifted high in the air and hurled over the brink and down into the canyon. The pilot's wife was standing outside and saw the whole thing. She sent word to us that our father had been killed. I was thirteen and Marla was only seven. We couldn't comprehend it at first. Our father was gone forever. We would never see him again. That was a sad day for the Bojeon household. I think our handyman Barney took it as hard as any of us. He and my dad had been best friends for over twenty years. I remember trying to go to sleep that night. I kept hearing Mom and my sister crying in the next room. A very sad time for us." Roselyn reached and rested her hand on his arm.

"Tropas, that is such a sad story. I am so sorry for you."

"I still think about Dad. He should never have stepped into the Death Zone. He knew better. It was just a poor decision, and he paid the price."

"I've always heard that working down at the Canyon

is considered the most hazardous job on the ark," said Hanley. "And I believe it."

"It's true," said Tropas. "Little Canyon is the most dangerous place on ***Proteus***."

"It's because of those damned wind-vanes," said Jerome. "They'll kill ya."

"They are lethal," said Tropas. "But the correct term is 'wind-*bane.*' "

"I don't know that word," said Roselyn. "What is a wind-bane?"

"It's a long, swirling, twisting length of wind," said Jerome. "It'll grab you and toss you up in the air."

"Right," said Tropas. "It's a long wind funnel, like a tendril. Some are hundreds of feet long. They're like dangerous wind snakes waiting to catch you, and they live close to the edge of Little Canyon, right at the brink."

"I went down to the Canyon once," said Hanley, "with some friends. There were a lot of tourists there that day. The security fence is a hundred feet from the edge and runs for miles, I guess. They won't let you inside. It's a noisy place. You can hear the wind howling and moaning, but there's also a weird sound that comes from down deep in the canyon itself. It's like a crunching, growling, grumbling roar, like some evil monster chained at the bottom."

"No one knows what makes that noise," said Tropas. "It's the sound of the cylinder mechanism as it revolves against the ark's outer shell. No one has gone down there for centuries."

"But why is the wind such a problem?" asked Roselyn. "I've never been to Little Canyon. All I know is what they taught us back in elementary school, and I remember being very confused about it."

"It has to do with the ark's gravity, right Tropas?"

"That's correct, Jerome, and the fact that the ark's two cylinders spin around so fast."

"About two hundred miles in one hour."

"Actually, its 225 miles. The cylinders complete about eleven revolutions in one hour. Another way to look at it is that each cylinder turns and comes back to the same spot about every five minutes."

"That's moving along damned fast," said Hanley.

"But why does the cylinder have to spin so fast?" asked Roselyn.

"That's where we get our gravity, sweetheart," said Jerome.

"Correct," said Tropas. "What we're feeling right now is artificial gravity. It's called centripetal force being exerted on us as we spin, and it's what holds us to the surface of the cylinder. That way, we don't go floating off in zero gravity."

"The guys who built this ark were pretty damned smart," said Jerome. "They calculated that both Alpha and Omega would have to rotate eleven times in one hour in order to duplicate the gravity that people on ancient earth felt."

"I feel so stupid," said Roselyn. "I guess I learned all this back when I was in elementary school, but it's slipped away over the years."

"Don't worry," said Tropas. "A lot of things, we just take for granted without realizing how they actually work."

"And this gravity stuff can get pretty damned complicated," declared Jerome.

"But I still don't understand why the winds are so bad at Little Canyon," said Roselyn. "Strong enough to kill people if they get too close."

"Little Canyon is only 50 feet across," said Tropas.

"Not very bright!" remarked Amhearst, still stationed at the stove and stirring his glop, but obviously tuned in to the conversation. "Why do you think they call it 'little,' dear Roselyn?"

"It's where the two cylinder edges meet," continued Tropas. "But Alpha and Omega are spinning in different directions, clockwise and counterclockwise."

"That's so that ***Proteus*** can travel straight ahead and not be pulled to one side or the other," said Jerome.

"True," said Tropas. "It gives the ark stability. But think about what this means for the Little Canyon. You have two cylinder edges only 50 feet apart and moving in opposite directions, and both spinning at 225 miles per hour. This makes the air between them go insane. It creates wind-banes and whirlpools of air, invisible tornadoes that grab you and spin you around and then hurl you down into the canyon, where the cylinder mechanism probably grinds you to pieces. That's why the ground on both sides of the canyon for a hundred feet is called the Death Zone. That's why a security fence is there to keep visitors from wandering into this space. They have warning signs posted up and down the fence. There are fence guards on duty all the time to keep people out. That was my dad's job."

"But in spite of all these measures," said Hanley, "people still walk into the Death Zone and end up dying."

"I hear that at least a dozen people die there every year," said Jerome. "It's the most popular tourist spot on the ark. Folks love to go there and crowd around the fence to hear the wind howl and the canyon speak. Then some drunk teenager climbs through the fence cables because his buddies dared him to. He scuttles out into the Zone and the wind picks him up before he can run back. It happens more often than you'd think."

"*People are such stupid cows!*" sang out Amhearst. And then in lower tones, "And I know a few."

15

He was only a few feet from the hall intersection when he heard the sounds. Tropas had left the kitchen and was on his way back to his quarters. He would rest there and relax till his noon meal run. Then he heard the sounds from around a corner just ahead. *Whap! Whap! Whap!* Someone wielding a whip. And after each punishing stroke, a wincing grunt of pain from the victim.

He stopped and peeked around the corner. Thirty feet down the hall, a young man knelt on the floor, his arms splayed out submissively. Tropas recognized Babson, one of the new orderlies he had met yesterday morning at the orientation session. A mop and bucket stood against the wall close by. Babson had been assigned janitorial duties. His job was to mop the hardwood floors in this section of the building. But something was terribly wrong! Babson had committed some heinous sin, because standing over him was Dr. Strabo himself. And the man was laying into the youngster with all his might. He wielded the dreadful white cat and lashed without mercy, the knotted cords biting into back and shoulders. Babson knelt meekly, without protest. He was allowing the beating to continue, enduring it as if he knew he deserved it.

Tropas was aghast. This was evil beyond evil. How could any moral man inflict this kind of savagery on another human being? No one deserved this manner of punishment, regardless of the offense. But of course Strabo was not a moral man. He was a degenerate animal engaged in his favorite pastime—doling out pain. Tropas recalled his sister's estimation of Brian Strabo: *He likes to hurt people.*

"We do not allow careless work at this institute!" growled Strabo, as he struck again and again.

"Yes sir," he sobbed. The boy was struggling to hold back tears. "It won't happen again. I promise."

"Maybe this will help you remember!" He hit him one final vicious blow. Babson flinched and cried out. "Now get up and finish your work. And if you leave one more spot of dirt on this polished hardwood, you'll get another dose of the cat. I'm coming around later to inspect these floors, and they'd better be spotless. *Now get to work!*" Strabo tucked the white cat into his belt, turned, and stalked off down the hall as Babson crippled to his feet and took up his mop.

So Babson got a savage beating for careless mopping. He left a dab of dirt and it netted him a dozen whip blows from this sadist—and only his second day on the job. This was insane! Strabo was a torturer who loved to inflict pain on meek underlings, those who would not fight back. And what would have been the outcome if Babson had rebelled? If he had been a man instead of a timid rabbit, what would it have got him? He would have lost his job and maybe would be facing trumped up assault charges. Strabo was powerful. He was vengeful and clever. If Babson had fought back, had knocked Strabo to the floor, as he should have, when he came at him with the whip, the boy might have been sentenced to time behind bars. Babson realized this. He needed this job. This was why he chose to endure the punishment—a perhaps smart but painful choice.

Tropas could not get past this episode he had witnessed. It haunted him, gnawed at him, throughout the morning. He was struck by the baleful contradiction—a meek, harmless lad savagely beaten, beaten for no good reason, by a sadistic monster posing as a medical doctor, someone dedicated to alleviating human suffering. The irony of it fairly screamed. No, Tropas would not soon forget what he had seen, and he would never look at Strabo again with the same eyes.

He was sitting quietly by the hearth, a thick book in his lap, when he heard the sound. It was shortly before midnight, Tuesday evening, and he had just begun reading an ancient play called *Macbeth*, penned eons ago by

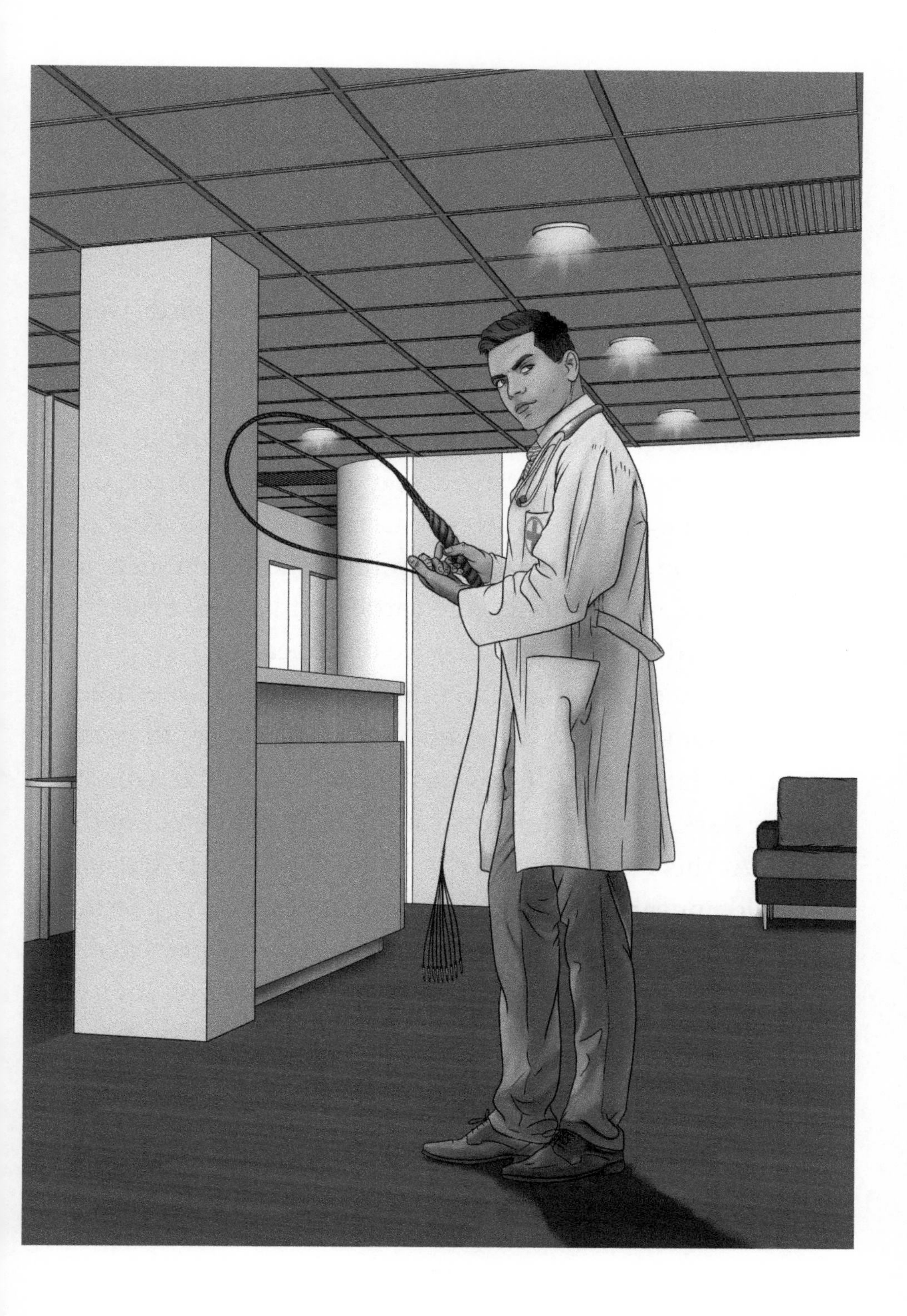

a famous playwright William Shakespeare. *Plop!* The sound came from his front porch. Something had fallen. Thaddur Kline put his book aside, rose, and went outside. Lying on his porch was a dead bird—an owl, a night bird. It had died while in flight and fallen onto the porch. The skies had been empty in recent days. The birds were gone. Kline had discovered many dead scattered about in his gardens. They simply died and fell.

Some evil had been spawned on ***Proteus***. It was stealing about among them and growing stronger day by day. The animals of the ark were dying. Kline kept no livestock on his little patch of ground, but he had seen his neighbors' stock perish—the cattle and horses, even the domestic dogs and cats, all were disappearing.

He gazed off in the direction of Murlington, five miles away. Some nights, if the air was clear, he could make out the faint glow of the metropolis, alive and vibrant after dark. But on this night his eyes could detect nothing. At this late hour, the city had gone to sleep. Or so it would appear. But standing in the darkness and peering into the distance, the man could feel a mighty presence, a dire evil, moving toward him like a massive wave, soon to engulf him and all others. An unwholesome pulse of corruption spreading from the city and washing over him as he stood in the gloom. A precursor of worse things to follow. "By the pricking of my thumb," as his mind turned to Shakespeare, "something wicked this way comes."

Abruptly, he thought of Marla. He could see a dark shroud stretching out to envelop her. The girl was in grave danger. He could not yet comprehend the source of her peril, but he knew the threat was real. From the depths of his soul, he sensed a danger. It cried out to him. Her life hung in a precarious balance. He loved this young woman. He would freely give up his own life to protect hers, and now he must go to her and warn her.

In a few hours it would be light. He would wait till dawn and then make his way to the Bojeon farm two miles distant. As he went back inside, he realized that after tomorrow, he might never return to this home again. He had built this house and this farm with his own hands. It was his. But the world of the ark was changing. Some unspeakable evil had been let loose and was fast approaching. He would have to flee and help others do the same. These were his thoughts as he lay in bed to try to snatch a few hours rest.

Barney had gone to bed by the tenth hour, but not to sleep. His eyes were open, and his mind refused to shut down. He could not get the day's events out of his head. His friend Casper had told him terrible things—people were dying in the city from some plague; hundreds were fleeing for their lives or else locking themselves in their homes. Stores and shops all closed, businesses shut down, strange black creatures roaming the streets and alleyways. What did it all mean? Casper was running away from this danger, and he had advised Barney to do the same. "Your family's farm is too close to the city. All of you are in great danger. You need to get farther away." Had this been his warning? Barney was confused. He had not yet shared any of this with Gabriella or Marla. What would they think? *You're overreacting, Barney. You need to calm yourself and think clearly. What goes on in the city is not any of our business.* These would be Gabriella's words to him. But what if the danger was real? And what was that black thing he had seen in the alley? He was truly scared. *I wish Tropas would come back home. He'd know what to do.* He pulled the blanket up under his chin, shut his eyes, and tried to drop off to sleep.

16

Curious eyes peered at her as she slipped into the hall and softly shut the door behind her. She was watched as she scurried away toward her own quarters, her nightgown fluttering. It was Wednesday morning, the sixth hour, and Helena Gimbal rushed to dress and prepare for the day. Then she must quickly seek out her friend Roselyn and tell her secret things, urgent things.

The day's work was underway when Helena stepped into the kitchen. She beckoned to Roselyn to come sit with her. She had important news to share.

"Day before yesterday, I was in the office and I overheard the doctor tell Tropas, the new guy, that he was to bring his sister here for a visit. Her name is Marla. It was something about Dr. Snyder needing to talk to this girl and I suppose get some information from her that he needed for his project. But there was something odd about what I heard. Brian seemed just a little too eager for this girl to come here. It was like they needed her for something special, but he wouldn't say what. So I decided to do some probing on my own. I spent last night with

Brian. We drank and stayed up late talking. He did most of the talking. I just kept filling his wine cup and asking him questions about this girl and Snyder's pet project. He kept giggling and talking and making me promise I wouldn't tell anyone the 'big secret.' Roselyn, he told me some horrible things that he and Snyder are up to. You wouldn't believe what he said. I'm not sure if I believe what I heard. I think he and Dr. Snyder are both maniacs, crazy men!"

"What did he say to you, Helena?"

"I can barely put it into words, Roselyn. They intend to take something from this girl. But if they do, it'll kill her." Hanley and Jerome stopped their work to listen. "How did Brian put it? They plan to 'harvest her ovaries.' Yes, that was the phrase he kept repeating over and over, and laughing like it was some kind of sick joke. He and Snyder intend to 'harvest her ovaries' and remove all her sex organs."

"That's really sick," said Hanley.

"They can't do that kind of surgery," said Jerome. "That would kill the girl. I think Strabo was just teasing you, trying to see how gullible you were."

"Right," said Hanley. "Maybe he wasn't as drunk as you thought he was."

"No, I think he meant it," said Helena. "I think that's exactly what they plan to do."

"Why would they do such a thing?" asked Roselyn.

"It's worse than sick. It's unholy."

"*Harvest her ovaries!*" sang out Amhearst, as he stirred glop.

"Please be quiet, Amhearst," said Roselyn. "We don't need to hear that repeated."

"Well, we need to get word to Tropas right away to keep his sister from coming here. She's not safe," said Helena. "When we see him, we need to tell him this. Don't bring her here."

"He should go back home at once," said Roselyn. "His whole family needs to relocate for a while. Go into hiding in case they try to come after her."

"That's the truth," said Jerome. "Snyder's a bigwig and he has powerful friends on the Council. If he can get them to declare this girl an 'Ultimate Asset,' then they'll send out marshals to go find her and bring her in for her 'protection.' Then they'll just turn her over to Snyder and Strabo, and the game will be over."

"True," agreed Hanley. "Snyder knows how to get what he wants. If Tropas balks at bringing her here, then they'll just take him out of the picture and go after the girl themselves."

"What's going on here? Why aren't you people working?" Loud, authoritative voice. Strabo stood in the doorway and gazed around the kitchen. "Miss Gimbal, don't you have work to do in my office? Why are you here chitchatting with the kitchen help?" Helena jumped up, edged past Strabo, and hurried down the hall toward her office. In a moment, she spotted Tropas coming toward her, on his way to the kitchen to pick up his first food cart of the day. She grabbed his arm.

"Tropas, you have to go home at once to look after your sister. Keep her away from here. She's in great danger."

"Helena, please calm down and tell me what's going on. What do you mean Marla's in danger?"

"The doctors want her for their experiments. They intend to perform surgery on her. She'll die if they get to her. You have to hide her before they send marshals out to pick her up. Take her someplace safe, out of their reach."

"You're not making sense. Is this a joke, Helena? How do you know all this?"

"I was curious about why Dr. Strabo was so eager for your sister to come here. I heard him talking to you in the office. So I stayed with him last night. He got drunk and told me everything. I'm not sure why, but they're gonna operate on your sister to remove her ovaries. I know it sounds grotesque, but that's what he said and I don't think he was lying. He's down at the kitchen right now. You shouldn't let him see you. You need to slip away and rush home and look after your sister." Tropas stood a moment staring at the woman. He was trying to process this new information. It was just too bizarre to grasp. *They want her here so they can . . . remove her organs? Because she's a skimmer? Use her for their sick lab experiments, like they've been using the isolation inmates? This is something out of a nightmare. But what if it's true? It would explain why Strabo wants her here so bad. And Snyder is going to have marshals sent out to pick her up? He could do that. He has pull with the Council. No, I have to go home. I can't take any chances with Marla's safety.*

"Thanks, Helena. I'm in your debt." He bent and gave her a quick kiss on the cheek. Then he turned and fled up the hall, heading for the front.

Brian Strabo was in his element, puffed up in his own conceit. He strutted slowly past Amhearst to pause a moment and watch Hanley busy with his cleaver, chopping tripe.

"Careful, young man," he snickered. "You don't want to lose one of your fingers." Suddenly Amhearst blared out in a schoolyard chant, "Harvest her ovaries! Harvest her ovaries!" repeating over and over. Strabo spun around.

"Why are you saying that, you idiot? Where did you hear it?" Amhearst ignored him, kept stirring the simmering glop cauldron, and continued chanting the phrase. "*Stop it, you moron!*" he shouted. But Amhearst would not. Strabo grabbed his shoulder, turned him, and slapped him hard across the face with an open palm. Amhearst did not react; he was silent. He simply gazed into the doctor's eyes and smiled.

"Hey! Leave him alone! He's not hurting anyone." Hanley had laid his cleaver aside and turned to confront Strabo.

"What did you say to me?" Anger building.

"I said leave off with the rough stuff."

"Yeah," said Jerome. "We don't like to see our friends hurt." Strabo's rage boiled over.

"How dare you talk to me like that! You're nothing but insects! I could have all of you fired . . . (finger snap) . . . like ***that***! You're all expendable!"

"I believe I'm the only hovercraft pilot on staff," said Jerome. "Perhaps that gives me a bit of an edge."

"*You imbeciles!*" He drew the white cat from his belt. "I'll give you an *edge*!" As he raised his weapon, Amhearst stepped to him from behind and seized his wrist. With his other hand he wrenched the cat loose and tossed it on the floor. Strabo was livid.

"*What are you doing, you fool?*" he screamed. "*Get out! You're fired! You don't work here anymore!*" Amhearst stepped close, reached up, and laced his fingers behind Strabo's neck.

"You sleep with her." The remark stopped Strabo. For a beat, he was confused.

"What do you . . . ?"

"I saw her leaving your bedroom."

"What are you talking about?" Amhearst drew the doctor's face to his and kissed him hard on the mouth.

"*Stop it, you idiot!*" he sputtered. He struggled to get free from the other's grasp. Amhearst brought his arms down over Strabo's shoulder and back, fingers still laced tightly. He pinned the doctor's arms and wrists against his waist. Strabo fought to free himself, but to no avail. Amhearst's arms formed a band of steel around the torso, hugging the doctor's frame tightly against his own body. He was a prisoner locked in this creature's embrace. Amhearst's expression never changed. He gazed up into the doctor's eyes and smiled serenely, as though thinking delightful thoughts, remembering pleasurable times. Hanley and Jerome looked on, but did not move.

Amhearst began his maneuver. He stooped slightly and then lifted Strabo a few inches off the floor. He eased over in front of the glop cauldron and stopped. Then slowly, slowly he leaned sideways, bringing Strabo's head closer to the large pot. All the while, the doctor struggled and yelled. He was helpless in Amhearst's mighty grasp. His legs were free, and he twisted and flailed and tried to bring his knees up. But it did him no good. He was trapped. Amhearst paused in his maneuvering and looked across the room toward his companions. He spoke out loudly.

"Gentlemen?"

"I think he wants us to help him," said Hanley.

"Oh well, why not?" observed Jerome. "It's been a slow day."

The two moved to join Amhearst. Hanley bent and

grabbed Strabo's feet and ankles, while Jerome took hold of the hips and thighs. Both lifted manfully and brought the doctor's frame up to horizontal. Inch by inch, they moved him closer to the stove and to the simmering cauldron. Amhearst positioned Strabo's head directly over the bubbling glop. Then the three men began the final stage. The legs were lifted high, while the head dipped lower. The doctor was positioned almost vertically directly over the surface. He choked as the fumes bathed his face. He continued to struggle and scream. "*No! No! No! Don't! Please don't!*" Lower, lower. He screamed out in agony as his scalp touched the simmering porridge and sank into it. Lower, lower, the three held the man subdued and helpless as they dipped his head on into the boiling glop. His screams turned to burbling whimpers and desperate grunts as the head disappeared up to the neck into the thick soup. They held him as his body convulsed and trembled. After a time his movements stopped and he went limp. The three kept him under another few minutes till they were certain he was gone. Then they brought him up. Hanley set the feet on the kitchen tile, while Amhearst hooked his chin over the cauldron's rim. The three stepped back to observe their handiwork. For a few seconds, the body remained still, the derriere jutting out at an obscene angle, arms dangling, and head balanced on the cauldron's edge. Then slowly, the corpse slid onto the floor. The head came down solid on the tile, creating a glop halo around the cranium.

Roselyn had remained against the far wall during this perverse execution. She had not moved. Her hands pressed against her mouth, with her eyes wide and frantic. Now she stepped forward and spoke.

"Hide his body in the cold storage pantry. Then go bring a mop and bucket. We have to clean up this mess before someone comes in and sees it."

"We'll get the ghoul squad to take his body out tonight and bury it," said Hanley. Roselyn shook her head.

"No, this is our little secret. No one else must know what happened here. You and Jerome will be the ghoul squad. You'll bury him out back late tonight. Put him out there with the other corpses."

"Should we pour out the glop and make a new batch?" asked Hanley.

"No point in wasting good glop," answered Jerome. "If the pukes detect a soupçon of new flavor, they'll appreciate the change and eat hardy."

17

By the eighth hour Tropas had managed to wave down a ride. A farmer hauling his produce to Murlington stopped to let the man climb onto the el-truck's flatbed. There he sat among a dozen baskets of vegetables and endured the bumpy journey into the city. He stepped down onto city pavement at twenty minutes past the eighth hour.

He knew that the quickest way home was to go into the city, get a hire carriage to take him across town to the forest road, and from there he had the familiar two-hour hike back to the Bojeon farm. He should be home by midmorning. But as he looked up and down the street, he quickly realized that something was very wrong. There was no movement, no activity. The city was dead. He would have to go across town on foot, and this would take several hours. Where were the citizens of Murlington? What had happened here? He set out, pacing swiftly along the sidewalk. He had no choice. He must get home as soon as possible.

As he walked, the feeling grew, like a sinister dark

cloud growing and engulfing him. He felt threatened. Danger lurked all around him, though he saw nothing. But he could feel it; he knew something was out there. Evil eyes were watching him, and his heart beat faster. He quickened his pace. Suddenly he heard the sound—a high yelp, an animal cry, a single burst followed by silence. Where had it come from? He couldn't tell, but it was close, perhaps a street over. Someone, or some thing, was following him, watching him. He detected movement. He peered across the street at the black beast crouching beside an el-truck. The ape-like animal shifted back and forth on its haunches and uttered strange gibbering sounds. Tropas realized that the thing was staring at him, sizing him up, through blazing red eyes, though it made no movement toward him. The man walked on, praying that the thing would not follow him. He knew not to run, lest it trigger an attack. Presently, a second beast emerged from around a corner and joined his companion by the truck. When it spotted Tropas, it emitted a piercing yowl, and both animals began a bizarre bouncing dance there on the sidewalk. Tropas walked on, never slowing. After a minute he glanced over his shoulder. The black things had disappeared. He shuddered and almost stumbled in his haste. He was trembling, fighting off panic. *What are those things? Where did they come from? What have I got myself into? Where is everyone?*

These questions tumbled through his mind as he hurried along. *I have to keep moving. I have to get home. Get away from the city! Don't panic! Don't panic!* But his hands shook. His whole body trembled. He was terrified to the core, for the first time in his life, beyond memory.

He strode along as fast as he could without breaking into a run. He had to conserve his energy. If he gave in to panic flight, he would soon tire and be at the mercy of those things, should he encounter them again. No, he must keep his head and just keep moving forward, keep walking. Another three blocks and he began to calm himself. Maybe the danger was past. He breathed deeply and was able to relax a bit. And then he heard them—a chorus of yips and yowls and obscene animal noises. He looked behind him, and there they were! Dozens of the creatures had come out of hiding and collected in a veritable mob only a city block from where he stood. They yelped and screamed and appeared to be eyeing him. But none moved toward him. They held their distance and jumped around and gave out with their cries. Some raised their arms and shook their fists. Many stooped and bounced on haunches. *They look like wild apes or baboons*, thought Tropas. *They look mad enough to kill. So why don't they attack?* As he turned to hurry on, Tropas almost tripped over the man. A thin, ragged gentleman had emerged from a recessed overhang in front of a shop entrance. He came out and squatted on the sidewalk directly in the other's path.

"Hey! Watch where you're going, friend!" Tropas jumped back, startled.

"Sorry. I didn't see you." He stood a moment staring at this new player. The man wore rags and was clearly in desperate need of a good bath. *He looks hungry. This poor fellow hasn't eaten in a while*, thought Tropas. But what was he doing here, out in the open, while the black beasts were roaming the streets? He didn't appear frightened.

"You got anything to eat on ya? I ain't had a bite in two days."

"Sorry, I don't have anything. But who are you? And where is everyone?"

"Ha! You must be new in town. They's all hidin' in their homes. They's afraid of the black fiends."

"And you're not? Why aren't you at home hiding like the others?"

"Brother, I *am* at home. The streets is where I live. I like it out in the open so's I can move around where I want. But sometimes I get awfully hungry. The black'uns has already eaten up all the free grub. Now a lot of 'em's goin' after the dead animals. Hell, the sons of bitches'll eat anything. I figure sooner or later, they'll settle on human flesh. It'll be either that or starve."

"And you're not afraid of them?" The man laughed.

"Not one bit. It's t'other way round. They's all afraid of *me*."

"But why? I don't understand."

"Watch this." He sat back and crossed his legs. Then he rose two feet into the air, spun around once, and hovered.

"You're a skimmer!"

"Damn right I'm a skimmer. And those bastards is skeered to death of me. I got a buddy over on Croth Boulevard. He's a skimmer too, and the black'uns stay clear of him like he was poison. Don't know why, but they jist don't favor us."

Tropas' mind was racing. This was something new. Maybe the beasts were staying away from him because they were cautious. He wasn't a skimmer, but his sister was. Maybe he carried the family gene, and these creatures could somehow sense it. A very intriguing theory, but he still wasn't out of danger. Of this he was certain. One last question he must ask this man.

"Where did they come from?"

"Dunno exactly. They's a disease goin' round that's killin' folks fast. But I think some of 'em, instead of dying, they change. They turn into these fiends. They ain't human no longer. All they want is to feed. They spend all the time lookin' for food, any kind of food. My notion is that sooner or later everybody in this city is either gonna be dead or turned into one of these animals. The people locked in their homes, they gotta come out after a time or else they'll starve to death. When they do, they either die of the sickness or they turn. It's gonna happen, my friend.

But by then I'll be dead of starvation. I know that for a fact. There jist ain't nothin' left around to eat."

Tropas pitied this poor wretch, but he knew there was nothing he could do to help him. And he had to continue on his way and hurry home to his family.

"I have to go now," he said. "Take care and good luck." He walked on. For the next hour all was quiet. He saw no more black beasts as he trudged across the city. By the tenth hour, he arrived at the zoo. It was deserted. Barney's friend Casper had left. As he passed the visitors' fence, he heard animal growling. Peering over the barricade, he saw two black beasts tearing at the carcass of some dead animal. They were snarling and challenging each other for the remaining flesh. Tropas could see that the animal—a lamb or goat perhaps—had been dead for several days. The carcass was decomposing badly, and the stench drifted to his nostrils. He had to move away quickly. But these black beasts were hungrily devouring the rotting meat. *Truly, they will eat anything. How soon before they discover that human flesh is also edible? But they avoid skimmers. This is good to know.*

He walked on, and soon the city with all its grief was behind him. He breathed clean air and felt renewed. Lacking any unanticipated hindrances, he would reach home by early afternoon.

18

"Hey, where's Tropas? Have any of you seen the new guy?" It was Wednesday evening, shortly before the sixth hour. Jester stood at the kitchen doorway. Hanley had made Tropas' morning and noon meal runs and was preparing to finish up with the final one of the day.

"He had to leave this morning, Jester. Family emergency." Roselyn, hard at work at the vegetable counter, had spoken. "I doubt he'll be back."

"That's too bad. I was beginning to like the old boy. We'll have to get a replacement. I'll check with Strabo. Any of you seen him today?"

"I'm afraid not," said Jerome. "I'm sure he's around here someplace." Amhearst broke into song.

First he's hot and now he's cold.

Pity he won't be growing old.

"Amhearst, we don't need your crooning," said Hanley. "Shut up and stir the glop."

"We can fetch Babson as a replacement," said Jester. "He's another new guy. Been mopping floors for three days. He might enjoy a promotion to food cart duty." He paused a second and stepped on into the kitchen. "Have any of you guys heard what's happening in the city? Or noticed anything weird going on here?"

"What do you mean?" asked Jerome. "The news we get is that a disease has broken out and a lot of people are dying."

"That's true," said Jester. "This sickness is contagious as hell and folks are dying by the hundreds. But the really strange part is that these black, hairy, ape-like things are running around loose. There are dozens of them roaming the streets, and they're eating everything. Nobody knows where they came from."

That sounds like bullshit," said Jerome. "Where did you hear this?"

"A buddy of mine goes to visit his folks there. He came back yesterday saying that the city is dead and these weird animals are prowling all over looking for food. People are leaving town as fast as they can. Another thing is that our work staff here is getting thin. Several orderlies have quit, and now you tell me that Tropas left too. Pretty soon we're gonna have to shut down the Institute and head for safer pastures."

"Don't know how we're gonna do that," said Jerome, "what with the pukes and all."

"I know, but what are you guys gonna do when the supplies run out? The animals are all dead. How are you gonna make your glop? What are we gonna feed the inmates?"

"For that matter," said Hanley, "what are *we* gonna eat if there's no delivery service, if we're cut off from the city? I think some hard times are ahead, and we'd better start preparing for the worst."

He arrived home at half past noon. From a distance he could see Marla sitting on the front steps beside an older man. Barney was pottering around the front yard. Coming closer, he recognized the man as Thaddur Kline. *What is Master Kline doing here? He's never visited our home before.* When his sister saw his approach, she jumped up and ran to him, giving him a warm embrace.

"Brother, I'm so happy to see you! But why are you home early? Is something the matter?" She took his hand as they walked. Thaddur rose to greet the boy as he approached.

"Tropas, you look well. It's good that you're back."

"You're always a welcome guest at our home, Master Kline. But I wish your visit came in happier times."

"He came to warn me and protect me, Brother. He feels that I am in danger."

"He speaks the truth, Marla. That is why I am here also."

"But why? What is this danger you both speak of?"

"Be patient, Sister. There is much to explain."

"Did you come through the city, Tropas?" Barney had stepped forward.

"Yes, and things are very different there now. I fear Murlington is dead. People are locked in their homes out of fear. Others are dying. There is a strange disease raging."

"And did you not see other things?" asked Kline. "I sense a great evil lurks there. It grows stronger each hour. I fear it will soon engulf us all if we do nothing."

"Yes, Master Kline," said Tropas. "I saw other things."

"Is that my son I hear?" Gabriella had appeared at the front door. "Welcome home, Son. You look hungry. All of you come inside and find seats at table. A nice noon meal is waiting."

Wednesday evening Helena stepped down to the kitchen. "Roselyn, have any of you seen Doctor Strabo? He's been missing since this morning, and several people have come by the office asking for him."

"No, Helena, we haven't seen him. He disappeared this morning right after you left."

"And what's even stranger, no one has seen Doctor Snyder since day before yesterday. Someone said he's locked himself in his private lab to work on his secret project. He doesn't answer when they knock on his door, and he doesn't come out to eat or anything. It's really weird."

Later, after midnight, Jerome and Hanley rose from their beds, found a shovel, and, as Roselyn had commanded them, performed their nocturnal task as ghoul squad. No one saw them come or go.

"The doctors were trying to get you to come to Swarthout. They were trying to lure you there and use you in their unholy experiments." Tropas spoke to the others as they sat around the table. "I told Doctor Strabo that I would try to bring you there next week, but of course that was a lie. I knew you would never agree to a visit. Doctor Snyder was desperate enough that he would have his friends on the Council of Elders send city marshals out here to pick you up and take you to the Institute."

"Why do they need me, Tropas? Why am I so special?"

"Because you're a skimmer. That has something to do with it, but I'm not sure what. Snyder needed you for his big project."

"I don't think any city marshals are gonna be comin' our way," said Barney. "I reckon they've got their hands full as is there in Murlington."

"You're probably right, Barney, but we can't take any chances with Marla's safety. I think we should leave here and find a safer place for a while, someplace out of harm's way."

"The lad is right," said Kline. "The greatest threat is not the city authorities. It is something else, some great evil that grows there. It is hungry. It will soon consume everything in this region."

"I know your meaning," said Tropas. "You speak of the black things. I saw them today roaming the streets, searching for food. There were dozens of them, maybe hundreds. They are mindless beasts, eating anything they can find, even the rotting animal carcasses."

"That's what my friend Casper was talking about," said Barney. "He said they was big hairy ape things prowling around. I think I spotted one in an alley."

"Their numbers have grown," said Tropas. "They are multiplying. Today I saw many, and they are starving. When they have consumed everything in the city, they will begin scouting out into the countryside. It's only a matter of time before they reach our farm. We have to leave here."

"Oh, this is insane," said Gabriella. "Are you men making this up? I think you're just trying to scare us."

"No," said Kline. "These things are true. We must leave and seek out a safer place—if there is one to be found."

"One thing odd about these creatures," said Tropas. "For some reason, they are afraid of skimmers. They stay far away from them. But I know that eventually, their hunger will cancel any fear they may have. None of us is safe."

"But where can we go?" Gabriella gazed at the others. "This is our home. There is no other place to run to."

"We'll find a place," said Marla. "We have to. We have no choice."

"If we can cross Little Canyon and travel into Omega," said Tropas, "we might be safe."

"Good thinking," said Barney. "I doubt the black'uns can follow us across."

"We can go to Omega D," said Tropas. "It's 50 square miles of forest. I'll wager we can find sanctuary there with some woodsman and his family."

"But we must leave quickly," said Kline, "as early as tomorrow morning."

"Pack up a few things, but not too much," said Barney. "We have to travel light. We'll head out at daybreak. Master Kline, you can sleep tonight in my shack. I have an extra cot."

19

Early Thursday morning, he stepped out of the hovercraft and began the trek across the quadrangle toward a rear entrance. He carried a small travel bag and moved cautiously, gazing down at the surface ahead of him. Those observing him thought he looked exhausted, a trifle haggard, feeble perhaps.

"It's Doctor Brownlee," said Jerome, peering out the window in the kitchen's back door. "He just flew in." The others crowded to see.

"He looks tired," said Hanley.

"I think he's lost weight," observed Roselyn. "I hope he drops by later for a visit."

Shortly after the eighth hour, Dr. Horace Brownlee stepped into the kitchen. He smiled broadly, glanced around, and waved to one and all.

"Welcome, Doctor Brownlee. Please come and sit with us. I'll get you some coffee." Roselyn hurried to fetch a cup and pour. Brownlee eased over and settled himself at the small table, as Roselyn set the cup before him. He placed his travel bag on the floor by his chair.

"Thank you, my dear. You're very kind." Hanley stepped forward.

"We saw you arrive, Doctor. We're glad to see you again. I hope you're doing well."

"Tolerable, lad, tolerable." He sipped his coffee. "These days, one does what he can and hopes for the best."

"May we ask about your visit?" Jerome had moved closer. "Are you taking a trip? I see you're carrying a travel bag."

"Don't be rude, Jerome." Roselyn frowned at him. "What Doctor Brownlee does is none of our concern." The doctor laughed.

"Quite all right, my dear. But before I explain my presence here, I'd like to offer a comment or two about the Institute. I've been walking around this morning exploring. I was told that about half the staff have quit and moved on. You're barely operating with a . . . what's the term? a 'skeleton crew'? Yes, that's it—a skeleton crew. You four here in the kitchen seem to be the strongest link in the chain of workers. I intended to speak with Dr. Snyder, ask him how he's getting on with his project, but apparently he's locked himself in his lab and refuses to come out. The man was once a brilliant geneticist, but I fear he's gone completely mad. Also Dr. Strabo seems to be missing. None of the staff seem overly concerned about that, however. So my conclusion is that Swarthout is facing its demise; this institute is enjoying its final days.

Such a pity! I was once proud to work here. But perhaps those who have abandoned their posts are the intelligent ones.

"Now to address your question, Jerome, yes, I am on a journey. I am leaving this area, and I won't be returning. An acquaintance will pick me up this afternoon and take me to the Little Canyon. From there I'll cross into Omega C and travel to the hamlet of Tarleton. I have friends there. I'll stay with them until we decide our safest course of action . . . if there is one to be found. I stopped here this morning to visit friends and to say goodbye . . . and to tell everyone that you also must leave. You must close this institution and abandon it very soon."

"But why?" asked Hanley. "What is happening?"

"We've heard rumors," said Jerome, "about terrible things going on in Murlington—diseases and dying and wild creatures roaming the streets. But truthfully, we don't know what to believe."

"I daresay all the things you've heard are true. But I doubt you realize the full impact of this catastrophe."

"What are you telling us, Doctor?" Roselyn eased into a chair and stared at the man. For a while, he said nothing. He looked down at his cup, as if choosing his next words carefully. He felt very tired, and Roselyn thought he looked very sad. After a time, he continued.

"My good friends, I cannot stress how serious our situation is at this moment. What has erupted among us may very well spell the end of us all. Our world on this ark may be coming to an end, and no way to prevent it. We all may be doomed." He paused to sip from his cup, now cradled in both his hands. Jerome smirked and quickly turned away to look at Amhearst, standing at the stove and stirring his glop.

"What you're saying is too incredible," said Hanley. "I can't accept it. Nothing could be as bad as what you're telling us."

"Doctor Brownlee, can you please explain this? Can you tell us more?" Little voice trembling, close to tears. She focused on the man sitting across from her.

"My dear girl, I wish I could be more optimistic. I wish I could tell you that there is still hope, some chance that we might escape what is coming. But this evil quickly approaching is so dire, so monstrous, that all we can do is flee from it and hope to survive for as long as possible. The thing rushing toward us is unstoppable."

"Doctor, could you maybe be more specific?" asked Hanley. "What is this 'thing' you're referring to? Does it have a name?"

"Indeed it does, my boy. It's known as Kestler's Syndrome."

"I've heard of that. Wasn't that the disease that almost wiped out the first ark travelers?"

"That's correct, Jerome. Kestler's Syndrome is what caused the Great Death two millennia ago. All children learn this bit of ark history in their elementary grades. The disease is quite virulent and contagious."

"But after that first outbreak, I thought it disappeared."

"No, Roselyn, it simply became dormant. It has survived these two thousand years, and now it has emerged once again, to our everlasting misery. The original ark travelers numbered only two thousand, but our population today has grown to twelve thousand. The catastrophe looming before us stands to be much more devastating. And to make matters even worse, the Kestler agent has mutated a notch over the centuries. Today's disease is triggering a bizarre side effect, and it is this strange quirk that poses the greatest threat to our very existence."

"What is this side effect, doctor? Please tell us everything."

"Hanley, my boy, you are wise to be concerned, even frightened. The demons that will soon pour out of Murlington are worse than any nightmare conceivable."

"Now you've got my full attention," said Jerome. "Could you please elaborate? Tell us about these demons."

"And why has this horrible disease suddenly woke up now," asked Roselyn, "after all these centuries? And where did it start? What was its point of origin?"

"You ask where did it first break out? The answer is simple, my dear. It crawled out of hibernation right where you and I are sitting. It emerged from the medical labs here at Swarthout Penal Institute."

20

"I'll tell you the unhappy story." Dr. Brownlee pushed his empty cup aside. "If any of us live through the ordeal that is coming, then perhaps there will be at least one soul who can pass along this bit of history to other survivors. The account must not be lost. Future citizens of ***Proteus***—and we must hope there will be some—need to know all the details, all the factors that caused the second Great Death on this ark.

"A year ago I worked here with Dr. Snyder in the Institute's research labs. I respected this man; I recognized his genius—one of the greatest geneticists ever born. He and I routinely performed autopsies on the inmates here who took their own lives. There were many. The miserable wretches locked in permanent isolation often saw suicide as their only means of escape.

"I recall the morning that Dr. Snyder made his first great discovery. In the brain stem of one of the suicides brought to us, the doctor found a strange substance. We extracted and tested it, and to our great surprise, we detected a tiny amount of the Kestler agent lying dormant in the tissue. The mysterious Kestler particle had always been one of Dr. Snyder's great interests. What was it? A virus? a bacterium? The ancient records never made this detail clear. And where had it gone after the Great Death subsided? Was it in hibernation, lying dormant somewhere? Was the little beast hiding from the outside world? These were questions that had obsessed Dr. Snyder all his life. And here was the thing itself lying dormant in the brain stem of one of the prisoners at this institute. The doctor carefully extracted and preserved the tiny sample.

"Time passed and other unfortunate inmates resorted to suicide. Their bodies were brought to us for examination. Dr. Snyder would dissect the brain stem—the proper term for this organ at the base of the brain is 'medulla oblongata'—and look closely for other traces of the Kestler agent. He found them in abundance. This was where the Kestler germ had been hiding all these eons. We extracted and carefully preserved these several samples. I assumed all along that the doctor intended to use them in some kind of future testing he had in mind. I never questioned his medical competence. Surely he knew how dangerous this stored material was, how disastrous it would be should anyone be accidentally exposed to the Kestler agent. These preserved samples were potential killers; they were dangerous beyond description. Yet the doctor was collecting them, hoarding them back, for some future purpose. I never voiced my concerns. I still had faith in Dr. Snyder's professional integrity.

"The second great breakthrough came the day the skimmer's body was brought to us. One of the criminals in isolation here happened to be a skimmer. I can't recall his name or whether he was a suicide or died from natural causes. But in any case, we were to examine the corpse. Oddly, we found no Kestler agents in his brain stem. This greatly puzzled Dr. Snyder. Why would a skimmer's medulla be free of any Kestler material? He decided to investigate this curious matter. For several days he ran tests, using some of the Kestler agent he had stored away. I remember the afternoon he came running out of his lab, exclaiming to me, 'I found it, Horace! I found it!' He had discovered that the skimmer's natural male hormone testosterone had a profound prophylactic effect on the Kestler germ. The organism was intensely allergic to this sex hormone. The doctor was hopping up and down with excitement. 'I think I can combine it with certain other compounds to produce a Kestler vaccine. We can banish the disease forever.'

"I thought this discovery was to be Dr. Snyder's crowning achievement, his life's glory. But two days later he came to me, beaming with even greater enthusiasm. He had been comparing the molecular structure of both the male testosterone and the female estrogen. He admitted that he was not one hundred percent certain, but was reasonably sure that the female hormone would prove to be vastly more efficacious than the male in preventing disease. When blended with certain compounds he had already developed, the estrogen from a female skimmer would combine to produce a powerful elixir, a miracle medicine that would prevent or cure not only Kestler's Syndrome but any and all other ailments. Also it might even reverse the aging process—allow an eighty-year-old man to be restored to the youth, vigor, and virility of a twenty-year-old. All that was needed was a skimmer's estrogen. However, it must come from a female of child-bearing age, ideally one in her late teens or in her twenties. But this effectively nullified his project. We both knew that female skimmers were rare in ark society. There currently were only three or four that we knew about, and none of these were in the proper age range. So his great dream died aborning. There was no goose to lay the required golden egg. He was forced to move on to more realistic projects.

"This was the point when Dr. Snyder's mind began to slip. He became fixated on the Kestler bug and the effects it would have on various creatures. He had a narrow cage constructed in one corner of his lab. He would not confide to me what its purpose might be, but I soon found out. One night he and Dr. Strabo went to the isolation cells and brought back one of the inmates. They anesthetized the fellow and while he was unconscious, injected him with the Kestler organism. Then they locked him in the cage. They did this as an experiment—to find out the effects that the modern agent would have on a human subject. Within 48 hours, the metamorphosis began. The subject gradually changed his physical form. He morphed into a black, hairy beast, a mindless animal driven by a ravenous hunger. He became one of the creatures that are now roaming the streets of Murlington searching for food. When I saw what Dr. Snyder had done, I quit my post here and took a job in the city medical center emergency ward. I saw no good reason to experiment on the inmates, to use them like laboratory animals. No benefit accrued from his cruel experiment.

"Dr. Strabo worked at the medical center on weekends, and he kept me posted on Dr. Snyder's activities. His next project involved using lower animals as lab subjects. For his own personal reasons, which I never fully understood, he was determined to find out how the Kestler particle would affect various mammals, amphibians, reptiles, and birds. For an entire month he had them brought in—farm animals, woodland creatures, a dog, cat, rodent, chicken, duck, and so on. He assembled a vast menagerie in the yard behind his lab. Most were kept in cages, some tied to posts, others in glass aquariums. His collection was quite extensive. While these creatures were being gathered, the two doctors went about replenishing the stock of Kestler material. There simply was not enough on hand to inject all the animals being collected. And this is the point at which my story turns very dark. The doctors began murdering inmates and extracting the Kestler from their brain stems. There is no other word for what they did. Dr. Strabo told me they killed seven prisoners over a six-week period. They would wait till after midnight to go fetch the man from his cell. They were very clever about it. They would wait till the viewing monitor was either asleep or absent from his post. Occasionally they would have him summoned away for a few minutes. Oh yes, they were very clever! No prying eyes ever witnessed their deeds. They would take the victim back to the lab and give him a lethal injection. After the surgery, they would arrange for the body to be secretly taken away and buried out back in the field. Dr. Strabo described this nefarious system to me in detail. I found his lack of compassion appalling. He rationalized their actions by maintaining that these inmates—I believe he called them 'pukes'—were the worst kinds of offenders, human scum, monsters, who deserved death. I disagreed, but did not argue too loudly. They were still human beings, and murder is still murder.

"The day arrived for the grand experiment to begin. Early one morning the two doctors began injecting the animals. They had accumulated enough Kestler to complete this task and were done before midday. Now the tragic chain of events begins. That same day, it seems one of the sweepers opened the door to Dr. Snyder's private lab and looked inside, just out of curiosity. The doctor caught him in the act and had him fired. Out of pure spite, this boy and some of his disgruntled cohorts came back later that night and released all the animals. This is the version that was told to me. The timing of these actions could not be worse. These animals, which were released and driven away, were the most dangerous creatures on the ark. Within 24 hours the Kestler took hold and they became extremely contagious. They went about infecting other animals, which in turn spread the disease to others, and so it went. Kestler has the effect on lower animals of deadening the voluntary muscles. They are paralyzed and freeze in place. The poor beast can't move. It becomes a living statue. After a day or so, it dies from hunger and dehydration. You've seen this happen already to all the animals in this region. Eventually all animals on the ark will die.

"The tragedy does not end with the removal of all our animals. Kestler has been released. It saturates the very air we breathe and spreads wildly. It ranks as the most contagious organism in the natural world. In all my years of medicine, I've never seen anything like it. At some point within the past few weeks, the Kestler agent jumped from animal to man. And this new mutated organism has the ability to transform. At first the infected victims expired quickly. Hundreds in Murlington died.

They were brought to the medical center, but we were unable to save them—not a single soul. But then the metamorphoses began. Instead of dying, the victim finds himself transformed. He is turned into a mindless, savage beast—a black fiend, if you will—driven by an insatiable hunger. These are the creatures we now are faced with, and their numbers are exploding in the city. The reason behind this strange metamorphosis is nebulous. My personal theory is that it is a survival mechanism. This new mutated strain of Kestler is desperate to survive. It wants its victims to live, so that they can go about infecting others and the disease can spread unchecked. Soon every human being in Murlington will become one of these fiends. Thousands will roam about in a desperate search for nourishment. But resources will disappear quickly. Eventually they must resort to consuming human flesh, our flesh, and then to cannibalism. Before reaching this stage, however, they will leave the city and go looking for food wherever they can find it. They will seek us out, kill us, and eat our bodies. We cannot avoid this. It is too late. All we can do is flee and hide and hope that in time, these creatures will feed on each other and die off. Maybe there is a chance that Kestler will retreat and go dormant once again. We can only hope and pray."

He ceased speaking and sat quietly, eyes lowered. All were silent, even Amhearst at the pot. After a time, it was Hanley who spoke.

"How much time do we have, doctor?"

"It's hard to say. A few days at most, but it would be risky to wait that long. I suspect a few of these creatures have already moved out of the city and are coming this way. If I were you, I would prepare to leave immediately. I think the safest course is to travel into Omega. I doubt the creatures can follow you there. The Little Canyon will surely be a formidable barrier. I hardly see how they can get across it. I'll arrive in Tarleton later this evening after dark. Perhaps you should come join me there. I would be happy to see you safe again, and we can plan our next move together." He rose and picked up his bag. "I must leave you now and go to wait for my friend. He'll be picking me up soon. Farewell to you all, and stay vigilant."

21

Tropas and his family rose early Thursday and prepared to travel. Taking only a few necessities and a little food, they were ready to begin their trek by the eighth hour. Their four-mile journey would take them across the neighboring pasture, through a section of forest, and on to Little Canyon, more or less in a direct line. Baring any difficulties, they should arrive at their destination—the closest canyon shuttlecraft launch site—well before noon. There they would rest a bit before crossing to begin the second leg of their journey.

"Are those shoes comfortable for walking, Mother?"

"They're fine, Marla. Don't worry about me. See to yourself. Make sure you pack everything you need."

The five stood before the big house and gazed around one final time before setting out on their long walk.

"This is our home," said Gabriella. "This is where you children grew up. Will we ever see it again after today?"

"Who can say?" said Tropas. "We might return someday. But for now, we have to think of the future and our own safety."

"And we must leave at once," said Kline. "We can't delay any longer."

"You got that right," said Barney. "Ms. Bojeon, you ain't used to walkin.' If ya git wore out, one of us'll carry you." Gabriella glared at him.

"Joke if you want. But I'll still be going strong when you and the others are dragging and lagging behind, Barney Grumb."

They shouldered their bags, turned away from home and life familiar, and set out across the empty field before them.

Shortly before the sixth hour, Thursday evening, Roselyn, Hanley, and Jerome made ready to leave Swarthout. Dr. Brownlee had painted them a dire picture of what was to come. He had advised them to get away for their own safety, and to do it soon. They had no reason to doubt this man. A nightmarish peril was fast approaching. If they lingered much longer here, they would all meet a horrible fate.

Jerome gave the Institute hovercraft a thorough preflight. He made certain its batteries were fully charged. They would take Amhearst, and the four of them would leave together. Their plan was to fly over the canyon into Omega C and arrive at Tarleton, the small village that was Dr. Brownlee's destination. Perhaps they would join him later that night.

Earlier, after Dr. Brownlee's departure, Roselyn had gone straight to her friend Helena and warned her to leave the Institute. She urged her to tell the other staff workers to get out also, though she had little hope that anyone would heed this warning. When Jester arrived to collect his evening food cart, Hanley took him aside.

"You have to get out, Trawley. Those hairy animals we've been hearing about are leaving the city and coming this way. You'd better pack up your things and run." Jester's reaction was to laugh.

"You have a wicked sense of humor, Hanley, old man. You really had me going for a second or two. All that talk we heard about black beasts roaming around Murlington was pure bullshit. Don't be fooled by everything you hear." Still chuckling, he rolled his cart away to go begin feeding his pukes their supper. Hanley saw that it was useless. Jester and the others would still be here, calmly going about their duties, when the horde of beasts arrived. They would be slaughtered. But what could he do? He turned and went back to join his companions. They would be leaving soon.

"We're ready to leave, Amhearst. It's time to go get on the hovercraft." Roselyn stood close to him as he calmly stirred his pot. He said nothing. "We have to go. We can't stay here. It's not safe. We want you to come with us." He stared into the cauldron and continued stirring. "Are you listening to me? We have to leave *now*!"

"I'm not going," he finally said.

"Why not?" asked Hanley. "If you stay here, the animals will get you. You'll die."

"I don't care. I'm afraid to fly. If I go up in the hubbercraft, I'll fall down."

"No, Amhearst," Roselyn pleaded. "It's safe to fly. You won't fall. Come with us. We have to go."

"No, Roselyn. I want to stay here. I have to stir the glop. I'll help feed the pukes."

"It's no use," said Jerome. "He's not coming. We can't wait any longer. Let's go."

"If Amhearst won't go, then let me run and get Helena. She can go in his place."

"All right, no reason to waste an empty seat. But hurry!"

At a quarter past six, the hovercraft lifted from its pad in the center of the quadrangle. Its four passengers would fly over Little Canyon and on to the village of Tarleton in Omega C, arriving by the seventh hour. There, with luck, they would join Dr. Brownlee, find lodging for the night, and begin making plans the following morning.

The exodus began in darkness early Friday, two hours before dawn. Thousands of fiends poured out of the city in a desperate quest for food. They scampered away aimlessly, tumbling over each other in their haste, yowling and bellowing, biting and gibbering. Murlington had been stripped clean. All stores of food had been plundered, all vegetation devoured. Even the leaves on the trees in the park were gone and the bark gnawed from ground up.

No human beings could be found anywhere in the metropolis. The hunt for human flesh had begun in the waning hours of the previous day. Doors were smashed; those few remaining in their homes hiding were mauled, ripped apart by savage teeth and claws, and then greedily devoured, some while still alive and screaming. The skimmers were the last to go—the two street beggars and the three elderly women hiding in their homes. All butchered without mercy and consumed.

In the early morning darkness, the starving black horde abandoned the city and raced out into the countryside. They targeted farms and dwellings still occupied by those who had naively ignored warnings to flee. But offerings were sparse. Only about a dozen victims were discovered, and these were quickly killed and eaten.

By dawn's early light, the black swarm reached Swarthout Penal Institute. The few remaining workers tried to flee, but they were trapped in halls and empty rooms. There was no place to run to. Jester heard the din and tried to escape through the kitchen's rear door. He raced across the quadrangle, three fiends in pursuit. He reached the hovercraft launch pad as they caught him. One bit into his neck, as a second disemboweled him. The third tugged at his arm till the shoulder snapped. The beast kept pulling till the arm tore lose. He took it aside, away from the others, and began feasting on the flesh and muscle.

Amhearst had risen early to start the morning's glop simmering. Upon hearing an uproar down the hall and getting closer, he paused to listen. Two black creatures suddenly appeared at the door. They stood a moment gazing at the figure holding a long wooden spoon, while it stared back at them. "Oh, shit!" he murmured softly. And then they were upon him.

Several beasts smashed open the door to Dr. Snyder's private lab. The delicious stench of rotting flesh assailed their nostrils, and they moaned with ecstasy. Across the room they saw one of their own crouched over a decaying mass of human remains. The black fiend was greedily gorging himself. Dr. Snyder had been dead for four days. The Kestler experiment had broken out of the cage and slaughtered his creator. Then it had fed on the corpse all week, its only source of nourishment. Dr. Snyder had sired this madness through his foolish preoccupation with Kestler. Now, by providing sustenance for this, his creation, he was perhaps reaping the reward for his own misguided labor.

The creature looked up from his putrescent meal and hissed at the others watching him from the doorway. Then they rushed across the room and all fed ravenously on the doctor's remains.

From their isolation cells, secure behind steel doors,

the pukes could hear the commotion in the halls outside. But they had no inkling of what was happening. Most wished the hubbub would go away. After all, it was almost time for breakfast.

22

They reached Little Canyon shortly before noon Thursday. Despite her earlier boasts, Gabriella Bojeon had not been able to keep pace with the others. She had had to hobble along the final mile through the forest and was completely exhausted by the time the group reached their destination. Marla and Tropas supported her the last quarter mile. Upon arriving at the canyon, they eased her gently onto the steps of the cabin near the security fence. The shuttlecraft pilot and his wife and small son lived here. Gabriella slipped her shoes off and began massaging her blistered, throbbing feet as a young woman stepped out of the cabin to greet them. Her small, three-year-old child stood close and clung to her. She smiled and nodded to the strangers, as she stooped and spoke to the little boy.

"Toby, I want you to go play in your sandbox awhile. You can play with your toys. Go on now." He scuttled down the steps and jumped into the box built onto the side of the cabin. The woman came down and extended her hand. "Hello, I'm Ireland Moss. You all look like weary travelers wanting to get across the canyon."

"That's correct, Ms. Moss." Tropas took her hand and spoke. "We're from up around Murlington. We've been walking all morning."

"Well, my husband's the pilot at this station, but he's not here right now. He went down to the commissary this morning for a few items. I'm expecting him back pretty soon. You all make yourselves comfortable." Then turning to Gabriella, "Darling, you look like you've had a rough morning. Here, let me help you up. Why don't we three girls go inside for a while? I'll make us some tea, and we can sit and chat a spell."

Two hours passed and the pilot had not returned. The huge canyon shuttlecraft sat silent on the nearby launch pad. Tropas stood with Thaddur Kline, and both men gazed at the vehicle.

"I don't like this, Master Kline. We're stranded here too long. We have to cross the canyon to safety. While we wait here, we are in great danger."

"This is true, Tropas. I feel a powerful enemy growing strong. Every hour the poison builds. It will soon burst forth and consume everything in its path. We should move at once. And the pilot and his family must come with us. Anyone remaining in Alpha is in great peril."

"How much time remains?"

"No one can say. Perhaps the evil has already erupted

from the city and is flowing toward us. We must stay cautious."

"There is a knoll a short distance behind this cabin. I think we would be wise to go there and observe. From the crest we should be able to scan a great distance—across the fields and the far edge of the forest we came through. If anything approaches, we will see it well before it gets here."

By the fourth hour, the pilot had not yet appeared. "I don't know what's keeping Herod." The young wife shook her head and gazed at the wall clock. "He should have come back by now." She and Marla still sat talking quietly. Empty tea cups rested on the table between them. Gabriella napped on the sofa. The wife rose and went to a window to look down on her small son, still busy playing in his sandbox.

Tropas and Thaddur Kline remained on the nearby hillock. They rested against a large rock and peered out across the open land, watchful sentinels ever scanning for any approaching danger. Neither had spoken for a long time.

Barney had walked a distance down the security fence. He stood a hundred feet from the cabin and leaned against a wooden post. He found himself enthralled by this ground, especially the sounds flowing out to his ears, the never-ending voice of the canyon as it spoke—the moaning of the wind-banes and the mysterious grinding, crunching, whirring noises emanating from the gorge. He relaxed against the fence post, his hands resting on the upper cable. The canyon noises became hypnotic. He was drifting toward sleep when he spotted the movement.

Little Toby was tired of sitting in his sandbox. He was bored with nothing to do. He climbed out and walked to the security fence. From a hundred feet away, across open, grassy ground, he could see the canyon and hear its noises. They meant little to him. They were the sounds he had listened to every day of his life; they were part of the normal.

Mom and Dad had warned him many times never to cross this fence. It was a very bad thing, a very dangerous thing, to venture out into the open area beyond the barrier. But no one had ever explained to him why this was such a great sin. After all, he could see clearly in all directions. There was nothing there that could harm him. He had often been tempted to disobey. He was a daring little boy, and today he was bored. Strangers had arrived; everyone had ignored him all afternoon. The urge grew strong in him to show off in front of these new people. It would be so easy to slip through the cables just this once, to go where he had been forbidden to go. He might be punished later, but right now Mommy wasn't looking. The thrill was just too tempting to resist. In the end, little Toby crawled through the cables and toddled out into the Death Zone.

Barney spotted the child when he had ventured about a third of the way to the canyon's edge. "Hey kid, get outta there! Whatta ya think you're doin'?" Toby heard the yelling and looked in Barney's direction, but never slowed his pace. The man slipped through the fence and dashed off toward the boy, nearly stumbling in his haste. Toby glanced over his shoulder and saw him coming fast. He laughed and toddled faster. It had become a game of chase. Barney caught the child, snatched him up, and turned to run back to safety. But they were now too deep into the Death Zone, more than halfway to the edge of the chasm. The man felt the vicious tightness across his chest as the wind-bane took him. He gripped the boy close and fought to get free. But he was no match for the canyon wind. He was lifted off his feet to hover helplessly in midair. Marla saw his plight. She had stepped outside and now stood gazing in horror as the man struggled in the throes of the lethal wind. Suddenly she lifted—higher than she had ever climbed before—and skimmed over the fence, racing toward the two. Ireland Moss stood on her front steps and stared in amazement. When she saw her son in grave danger, she ran to the fence and screamed out his name. As Marla reached him, Barney felt himself being pulled backwards. "Here, take him!" He thrust the child toward Marla an instant before he was hurled high in the air. She caught the little one safely and held him, but could do nothing to save her friend. She looked on in misery as the whirlwind spun and twisted Barney. He yelped and cried out as he was twirled like a top and turned upside down. Finally the malevolent wind flung him over the canyon's rim and down into the abyss. Marla heard his final screams as he fell into oblivion.

Still hovering and clutching the weeping child, she turned to take him to safety. But something was wrong! She could not propel herself forward. A wind-bane had gripped her, and she too was trapped in the currents. She struggled, but it was useless. Soon the two of them would also be cast down into the canyon depths to die. Suddenly, he was beside her. He had seen her dilemma and flown to her in a heartbeat. She felt a strong arm around her waist, tugging her away from the clutches of the wind. They were no match for his strength. The three sailed away from danger, passed over the security fence, and set foot on safe, solid ground.

Ireland seized her little one and knelt, clutching him to her breast and sobbing. "Don't you *ever* do that again! Do you hear me? You could have been killed!" She gazed up at Marla. "Oh, *thank you! Thank you!*" And then she wept anew.

"You saved me, Master Thaddur." Her arms went around him. She pulled him close.

"My dearest girl, don't you remember? I once told you that I would always catch you."

"I love you," she whispered, and then he kissed her.

Gabriella had come out of the cabin. She looked around at all the faces.

"Where's Barney?"

"He's gone, Mother." Tropas had answered.

"But where is he? Where did he go?" Marla went to her and spoke gently.

"He died, Mama. The wind pulled him into the canyon."

"He saved the little boy, Mother," said Tropas. "Barney was a good man, and today he was a hero." Gabriella collapsed onto the steps. She put her hands to her face and wept.

"Just like Joseph," she cried. "He left us just like Joseph." Tropas sat beside her, his arm around her shoulders.

"Barney was one of the finest men I ever knew, Mother. He'll always be with us."

23

Herod Moss, the shuttlecraft pilot, arrived home at the fifth hour. When he learned of the tragedy, he was shaken. "My son was responsible for a man's death? How could this happen, Ireland? Why weren't you watching Toby closer?"

"Why weren't you here to help me, Herod? I can't do everything myself."

"It was an accident," said Tropas. "Your son is just a little boy, and little boys sometimes do naughty things."

"Our being here was a distraction," said Gabriella. "We're as much to blame as anyone."

"No matter," said the father. "Toby did something we had told him many times not to do. He was disobedient, and because of this wickedness, your friend died unnecessarily. When my son gets older, I will certainly tell him how he caused a man's death today." Tropas cast eyes down and shook his head in sorrow.

"Mr. Moss, your son is only three years old. I am no father, but I suspect it's not unusual for small children to test the limits of their parents' authority. If you bring this up when he grows older, it will only cause him guilt and unhappiness. This little boy suffered severe emotional trauma that he may never completely recover from. Perhaps the best thing to do is help him forget today's happenings."

"You are very wise, Mr. Bojeon," said Ireland. "And your sister and her friend are the most amazing skimmers I have ever seen. They can fairly fly. Only someone with their ability could have rescued Toby. I will always be grateful for what they did." Then to her husband, "Why were you so late returning this afternoon, Herod? did you lose your way home?"

"I stayed with the others at the commissary. There was much talk about strange goings-on in Murlington. One of the men had just returned from there. He told us the city is dying. He talked about disease spreading and horrible hungry creatures roaming about. He said their numbers are growing and that all of us in Alpha should be fearful."

"These are true reports," said Tropas. "I have been in the city, and I have seen these creatures. They are huge, dangerous, ape-like things. Their numbers are indeed increasing, and soon they will quit the city and begin ravaging the countryside. No one in Alpha is safe. That is why we are here. We intend to cross over into Omega and seek refuge. And you and your family should come along too. I think the beasts will reach this spot within the next day or so."

"Where will you travel to after you cross?"

"We have no definite destination. Perhaps the forests of Omega D might be a safe place."

"We have friends in the hamlet of Tarleton. That is where we will go. You and your group should come with us. The people of Tarleton number about three hundred. We might be able to muster some kind of defense. There is strength in numbers."

Herod and Ireland Moss hurriedly packed their bags, and at the sixth hour, locked their cabin door and made for the canyon shuttlecraft. It rose from its launch pad with seven aboard. It quickly ascended to a thousand feet, the necessary altitude to avoid treacherous winds, crossed over Little Canyon, and after descending to match Omega cylinder ground speed, hastened on to Tarleton, a mere fifteen-minute flight for the powerful craft.

"Look, my friends from Swarthout are here." Tropas had climbed out of the canyon shuttlecraft and was staring at the vehicle parked close by. "You see the insignia on the fuselage, 'Swarthout Penal Institute.' This is the name of a prison not far from Murlington. I worked there only a day or two ago. This craft is their company transport. The pilot is a friend of mine. He works in the kitchen, and I'll bet the other kitchen workers came here with him. They are all my friends."

"Meeting your friends here would be a happy coincidence," said Herod. "Perhaps they fled here for the same reason we have. Let's get our luggage and go seek them in town. Many visitors to Tarleton can be found at the Coltsfoot Tavern this time of evening. Your friends may be there now. It is the best place to go for a good meal. And you can also find lodging for the night."

The Coltsfoot Tavern was the principal social gathering place in the village of Tarleton. Tropas could see that the building was very old, as were all the interior furnishings. The heavy tables and chairs within the main public area were dark and polished from years, possibly generations, of use. The place was bustling when he and his group entered. Scores of noisy patrons sat around dozens of huge round tables, while busy servers scurried about delivering food and drink. Tropas spotted his friends sitting around a table in a far corner and made in that direction. Jerome looked up as the group approached and beamed when he recognized Tropas. He jumped to his feet, hand extended in a warm greeting. "What a surprise! Tropas Bojeon showing up here after all this time."

"Hell, I was at Swarthout only yesterday morning, Jerome. Did you misplace your memory? And it's good to see Roselyn, Hanley, and Helena. Thank goodness you're all safe."

"We came here to *stay* safe," said Hanley, "same as you, no doubt."

"That's true. We just arrived. This is my sister Marla and my mom. The tall fellow is Thaddur Kline. I know you've heard of him. And this is Herrod Moss and his wife Ireland and their little boy Toby. Herod's the pilot who brought us here."

"We're all pleased to meet you," said Jerome. "Please, all of you sit with us. There's plenty of room at this table. Tropas, the bearded gentleman to my right is Dr. Horace Brownlee. He arrived earlier and joined us for dinner."

"There's someone missing," said Tropas. "Where is Amhearst?"

"He refused to come," replied Roselyn. "The poor soul is afraid to fly."

"I came instead," said Helena. "I am so thankful to get away from there."

"I don't know what will happen to Amhearst, Jester, and the others at Swarthout," said Jerome. "And what about all the pukes?" asked Hanley. "We're not there to make the glop. Amhearst can't manage it all by himself. The inmates will starve in their cells."

"So you all work at this prison," said Herod. "I hear bad things are gonna start happening up there soon. It's best we all got away. Maybe we're safe here in Omega. They tell me the evil critters can't get across Little Canyon."

"It's not the black fiends all of us here have to fear." Dr. Brownlee spoke up for the first time.

"What do you mean, doctor?" Tropas asked.

"True, the black creatures probably won't be able to cross the canyon, as you said, Mr. Moss. But the air is free to come and go where it will. Alpha air right now is saturated with Kestler particles. These germs are airborne and they are everywhere. They were spread first by the animals and then by the thousands who died and who are still dying from Kestler's Syndrome. I suspect the growing numbers of black fiends contribute to the pollution also. Each creature expels contagion with every breath it takes. It's only a matter of time before this contamination reaches us. The violent air currents at the Little Canyon will only intensify the problem. Massive quantities of corrupted air, I suspect, even now are being swept across into Omega. Soon we'll get word that the pandemic has broken out among us. And then the creatures will begin to appear. Nowhere on the ark will anyone be safe." A somber silence fell as the man's truth struck home. After a moment Helena rose from her chair.

"Everyone please excuse me. I'm going up to my room. I fear I've lost my appetite for this evening."

24

Early Friday morning, two men sat together at a table in the downstairs dining area of Coltsfoot Tavern. Several miles away, monstrous mayhem was afoot in Alpha; it poured out of Murlington and savaged the Swarthout Institute. While Amhearst and Jester were being ripped apart and devoured, Tropas and Thaddur Kline sat quietly over morning coffee and discussed their precarious situation.

"What is our plan, Master Kline? It is not prudent to sit and do nothing, but what can we do? Where can we go? We are short on options."

"This is so. There are no defenses here in this peaceful village. If the illness comes to us, as Dr. Brownlee predicted, all we can do is run and hide. And that is no solution."

At half past the seventh hour, Dr. Brownlee entered the tavern and came and sat. A young server set a fresh cup before him and poured coffee. Tropas and Kline sat silent, waiting for any report the doctor might have. At first he said nothing, only stared at the table before him while lifting his cup with trembling fingers to sip. Finally he looked up at the two men and spoke.

"It's happened. Kestler has jumped the canyon and is on its way to us. I rose up early this morning and went out to walk around the streets and listen for any news I might hear. Several black creatures have been sighted up near the canyon. I think their numbers will increase quickly. First a man, then a fiend, within a short time, perhaps hours. I believe the organism has mutated again. It doesn't kill now. That would be wasteful. No, it simply transforms, and it does this rapidly. Today a dozen beasts, tomorrow a hundred."

"But the numbers favor us," said Tropas. "The population is thin in this region—only a few farmers and settlers up around the canyon rim. Murlington was home to about eight thousand, densely concentrated, an ideal environment where Kestler was able to thrive and explode. But that is not the case in this area. Surely this must mean something."

"It only means that it might take a bit longer for disaster to reach us," said the doctor. "But now that it is here, it will surely spread. It's just a matter of time."

"Why can't we fight and kill these creatures while their numbers are few? Why must we cower back like the goat on the chain, put out to bait the wolf?"

"My brave boy, your courage is admirable. But we would lose. These are powerful, savage animals capable of great speed. They possess lightning reflexes, razor-sharp teeth and claws, and are driven by ferocious hunger, perhaps the strongest motivation in the animal world. No, they would quickly overpower us if we tried to fight them. We are their food. They will never leave off their pursuit."

"If the Kestler infection reaches this town," said Kline, "then the number of beasts will climb quickly into the hundreds."

"Ah, Master Kline, do you not know Tarleton's history? And you are a skimmer? I just assumed that all who have the power to lift held this village sacred. Tarleton is very old. It was founded over three centuries ago. It was during an era when skimmers were out of favor in the general ark population. During that ancient time, I believe there were only about 40 skimmers living, and they were looked down upon. That was an age of ignorant superstition. Skimmers were thought to be evil. Their gaze could kill you. They brought disease and bad luck. Many believed they should all be put to death. But the people living in the small community that would someday be named Tarleton were wiser than most. They considered the skimmer to be an ordinary citizen who possessed a unique gift, nothing more. Therefore, they welcomed skimmers into their midst. Tarleton became a mecca for all skimmers. They journeyed to this place to make their homes and live in peace. Today almost all citizens of Tarleton are descended from those early folk. There are only a few actual skimmers living here today, but almost all inhabitants carry the family gene, just as you do, Tropas. And the Kestler agent hates the skimmer. It is violently allergic to your hormones. You have permanent immunity against the Kestler organism."

"This is good to know, and I thank you for the history lesson, doctor, but it just means that no one in Tarleton will contract Kestlers and turn into one of these creatures. But everyone here, including myself, can still be eaten by the beasts."

"I think we should keep this bad news from the ladies for the time being," said the doctor. "There is no point in causing them anxiety before it is absolutely necessary."

"No, doctor, we share everything with them. They have a right to know the full truth, just as we do."

"Tropas is right," said Kline. "I know that Marla is strong enough to accept that danger approaches. She will not flinch."

At the eighth hour, a young man entered the tavern and sat a table away from the others. He wore a blue and gold uniform, identifying him as a member of the ark pilot/navigation crew. He looked over at the three men, nodded, and smiled. Tropas thought he looked tired. He noticed that his uniform was wrinkled and disheveled, as though he might have slept in it. After the young man ordered coffee, Tropas spoke up.

"Good morning. Care to join us?"

25

He set his cup down and took a chair beside the others, but said nothing at first. "I'm Tropas Bojeon and this is my friend Thaddur Kline." The young man was silent. "And who might you be?"

"My name is Rocco Palquy."

"I see you wear the uniform of Ark Control," said Kline. "Are you pilot or navigator?"

"I'm a navigator, as well as hovercraft pilot. Actually, I'm a staff astronomer. That is my specialty. I show the ark pilots where to go."

"We see few Controllers in this region," said Tropas. "May I ask, are you on a special mission?" The young man nodded and smiled weakly.

"Yes, I was on a very special mission." He paused and looked down at his cup before continuing. "But it's over now. It's all over. Everything is over." *Is this man about to burst into tears*, thought Tropas. *I've not seen anyone so sad.* He glanced quickly at Thaddur Kline before going on.

"Mr. Palquy, I can see there is something very wrong. Is there anything you want to share with us?"

Before he could respond, the tavern door flew open, and Herod Moss burst into the room, all in a panic. He dashed over to the three men and stood panting, struggling to catch his breath. Finally he was able to speak. "There are dozens of them and they're coming! They'll be here by tomorrow, maybe by tonight!" He paused to breathe.

"Mr. Moss, please calm yourself," said Tropas. "What are you telling us?"

"It's the forest people. They've all turned. It's been going on for days, all the folks in the little village close to the canyon. The Kestler got to them. Now they're coming for us and they'll be here soon. That's the word I hear."

"Our dilemma just keeps getting worse," said Kline.

"But what can we do?" Moss was still frantic. "Where can we go?"

"It doesn't really matter." The others stared at the man in the blue uniform. "You can stay here or you can run. It doesn't make any difference."

"What are you saying?" demanded Tropas. "Please tell us what you know."

"By this time tomorrow, our world will be over. This ark and everything we know, everything we've created, will come to an end."

"You're talking in riddles," said Kline.

"And you're scaring the hell out of me," said Tropas. "Can you please explain yourself?"

"Who are you?" asked Moss. "And what do you know that we don't?" Rocco Palquy began to weep. He struggled to speak, but could not for a time. Slowly he collected himself and dried his eyes.

"Sorry, gentlemen. I wish I didn't have to tell you what I'm about to, but you'd find out soon enough anyway." He paused to gaze at the three men around him. They saw him fighting to maintain his composure. "My buddy and I were supposed to get there and turn it on by midnight last night. But it never happened." He paused again, struggling to choose his words carefully. "It was a simple job. We had plenty of time. Then everything went bad. The anti-grav station is only a mile from here. It's the big steel blockhouse built into the Omega Great Wall. Nobody's been there for over ten years. It stays empty and locked. Ark Control has to use the anti-grav device only once or twice in a generation, if that often.

"Overall, we do a damned good job of steering ***Proteus*** through the cosmos. We almost never bump into things we're not supposed to. We avoid planets, stars, and black holes—objects with strong gravitational fields that could suck the ark in. A year ago we entered the Centris star system. Centris is a yellow star about the same mass as ancient earth's sun. It has five planets orbiting it. We've passed two and are approaching the third.

"A week ago we detected a massive asteroid belt in our path. We slowed the ark and considered moving through this cluster. But plans changed. Wisdom prevailed. It was deemed too risky allowing collisions, even though the ark's outer shell is tough. So we chose to steer clear. But this meant coming too close to the third planet, Centris-C. The solution was to activate the anti-grav. When the device is turned on, a quantum field surrounds the ark so that it's not affected by a planet's gravity. The gravitons just slide around the vessel. We planned to pass close to the planet, so as to avoid the asteroid belt. This would have worked great if we had managed to turn the device on.

"My friend Yipper Kolfack and I were sent out two days ago in the Ark Control hovercraft. We were to fly non-stop all the way to the aft wall and land near the anti-grav station. Yipper is an ark pilot. He's one of only three who know how to operate the device. I carry the entry codes and can get into the station okay. But I have no idea how the anti-grav device actually works. So we two set out mid-afternoon on what should have been a simple, easy mission. We had plenty of time to get to the device and turn it on. As long as it was activated by midnight of last night, all would be okay. But this never happened. Things began to fall apart almost from the beginning.

"Our first problem was hovercraft power. Someone had neglected to charge the cylinders. We had to stop at one of the Little Canyon shuttle stations to power up again. This shouldn't have been a problem—it shouldn't have taken more than three or four hours. We still had plenty of time. But while we waited, Yipper began drinking with the station pilot. He was an old codger who favored rice wine, and he didn't like to drink alone. So he and Yipper got drunk together. All was not lost because I can fly a hovercraft, and by the time we arrived at the AG station, Yipper would have sobered up enough to turn the device on. But then things went further downhill.

"When our hovercraft was finally ready to fly, it was half past the eighth hour and darkness had fallen. I urged Yipper to come along. I would fly the hovercraft the rest of the way. But he was still drinking and having a good time. The two drunk men walked over to the security fence and waited to see a static discharge. The old fool had told Yipper that a big, blue lightning bolt would soon jump across the canyon, and it was truly a beautiful and amazing sight to see. So they stood awhile to see the lightning jump. After an hour Yipper got impatient. He decided to walk out into the Death Zone to get a better view. The station master begged him not to, told him it was too dangerous. But Yipper was too drunk to use common sense. He walked out and the wind grabbed him and he died in the canyon. There was nothing I could do.

"When I saw this happen, I knew that everyone on the ark was in serious trouble. It was after the tenth hour. There was no time to fly back to Ark Control to fetch someone who could work the AG device, no guarantee that another pilot who knew how would even be available at this late hour. No, the mission was doomed, and I was alone. I flew the hovercraft to this little town and set it down beside two others. I was so miserable that I didn't even get out. I slept in the vehicle last night."

"What exactly are you telling us about the ark?" asked Moss. "Are you saying it's gonna collide with this planet we're coming up on?"

"That's precisely what's about to happen, sir. But 'collide' is the wrong term to describe what will take place. In a few hours from now, the planet's gravitational field will grab us. Our velocity will gradually increase, and eventually the ***Proteus*** will be hurled to the planet's surface. Our impact will be so great that nothing will survive. Everything will be vaporized; all living creatures will perish, large and small—down to the tiniest microbes and the bacteria under your toenails."

"How much time do we have?" asked Tropas.

"Difficult to say. I predict we'll begin to tilt toward the planet by this afternoon. Everyone will know that something is wrong. We'll impact later tonight. I can't set an exact timetable for these events. I just know that they will happen. The ark is doomed. All our lives are about to end, and there's nothing we can do to prevent it."

"At least it'll be quick and painless," said Moss.

26

By early afternoon a host of people were assembled in the Coltsfoot Tavern public room. Families had gathered. Conversations were intense. Few were able or willing to accept the significance of the young Controller's message—that their lives on the ark would soon be over, that there would be no tomorrow. The danger posed by the Kestler beasts now seemed trivial compared with the larger threat of ***Proteus***' total annihilation.

A crowd had gathered around the blue uniform. People hungry for more detail were asking the young man sundry questions, as if extracting new information would somehow diminish the awful threat. Rocco Palquy was dead-on-his-feet exhausted, but he patiently tried to answer all their questions. He knew these people were terrified, as well they should be.

Tropas stayed close to the Controller. An idea had been flirting with his imagination all morning, had been teasing its way into his thoughts, but he needed more input. Could there be some way for at least a few to survive? He must join the others and ask Palquy some questions of his own.

"Rocco, I'm curious about something. Why was the anti-gravity station placed where it was? Why put it at the very back of the Omega cylinder, the ark's most inaccessible spot?"

"As I explained earlier, Tropas, the station isn't used very often, almost never. The ancient builders considered the space closer to the bow more valuable. I suppose it's the same principle as tossing an item you seldom need or use into the back of your storeroom. Also this area of the ark is rather secluded. Less of a chance that some meddler might break into the station and tamper with the controls. That kind of mischief could easily turn into a disaster. The anti-grav device is quite powerful. So it was housed in a structure equivalent to a steel vault and placed in an area where few ever go. It sits on the boundary between Omega C and D."

"I understand. And I have one more question, Rocco. You say that now it's too late to avoid this planet Centris-C, that collision is imminent, that using the anti-grav device at this point would be useless. But what would happen if we turned it on anyway? Would it affect the ark's descent?"

"Clearly, this has never happened before, Tropas. I can only guess at the possible effect. Activating the AG would instantly cancel the planet's gravitational pull. But the ark would still plummet to the surface from sheer inertia.

We slowed the ark's velocity, but she is still traveling very fast. The AG would allow the ark to descend at a constant speed, with no gravitational acceleration. It might soften the impact somewhat, but the ark would still be crushed. We would not survive."

"Some of us might if we were locked inside the anti-grav station, which you describe as a 'steel vault.' The odds are small and the risk is great, but at least it's a chance for survival. It's a chance we must take, Rocco."

"Perhaps you're right, my friend, but your idea depends on our being able to turn the AG device on. I can't do it. I don't know how. All I can do is get us inside the station. Then it'll be up to you."

"Before last week I was a weatherman. I've put in my time tinkering with switches and dials. All I can do is try."

"If you're correct in your thinking and some of us manage to escape the ark's destruction, we might have a chance for survival on this planet. We ran an analysis of Centris-C. It's roughly the size of ancient earth. It has an oxygen-rich atmosphere and liquid water. It's the proper distance from its yellow star. There might even be intelligent life there, as far as we know."

"This is encouraging, but we haven't much time. We must go quickly. You say this AG station is only a mile from Tarleton? Let's gather our people and set out—and hope the Kestler beasts are still far away."

Tropas found the prevailing attitude among Tarleton

citizens discouraging. Many folk, especially the older ones, refused to believe Rocco Palquy's bizarre account. The young man was mistaken, lying, or just plain crazy. The ***Proteus*** had survived in space for over two thousand years, and it would continue on its journey another thousand. It was their home and it was indestructible. They had more immediate problems coping with the Kestler threat than contemplating a collision with a planet they couldn't see.

By late afternoon, Tropas, Herod Moss, and their families were ready to march. They had persuaded only 27 Tarleton citizens to go with them. At the fourth hour, the brave little band of 40 set out for the AG station a mile away. The oldest in the group was a 60-year-old gentleman. The youngest was little Toby Moss. Besides him, there were two other children, both under age twelve.

Tropas regretted the small number, but on the other hand, it might be good that there were no more than 40 souls. Rocco had implied that the anti-grav station was not a huge structure. For certain, it would not accommodate an overly large crowd of people. Tropas was praying that when they arrived, all these bodies would somehow fit into the building.

Tropas had become the group's unacknowledged leader. It was he who had hit upon this plan for salvation, desperate though it might be. This was his brainchild and he was the organizer. His determination to save lives was fueling their own hopes. All understood that when they arrived at the station, the AG device must be turned on for this plan to succeed, for there to be any chance for survival. And it was Tropas who must decipher the riddle. He must find the solution. If they were to be saved, Tropas would be the savior.

They said their good-byes and set out. They paced along quickly; few spoke. Herod Moss carried his son and walked at the head of the procession, along with Tropas and Rocco. The land between the village and their destination was largely flat ground, containing only an occasional tree or bush. There was good visibility in all directions. They were close to the Omega Great Wall. They could see it rise up into the cloud cover. The antigrav station lay only a short distance ahead.

"It feels like I'm walkin' downhill." Moss stared at the ground in front of him.

"It's the planet's gravity," explained Rocco. "The ark's bow is being tilted. In a few hours the effect will be more noticeable. The ***Proteus*** is literally being pulled toward the planet, bow first."

"I figure it's gonna get real nasty for the folks back in Tarleton," declared Moss. "In a little bit, the plates and cups are gonna start slidin' off the table onto the floor."

That's the least of their problems, thought Tropas.

By half past the fourth hour, they could make out the AG station up ahead—a large, square structure without windows, built up on an embankment, and apparently attached to the Great Wall directly behind it.

"There she stands!" crowed Moss. "Let's get to'er."

They swarmed up the embankment and crowded around the entrance, a heavy steel door. Rocco uncovered a keypad and punched in a series of numbers. A loud *clunk!* could be heard as steel bolts withdrew and the door edged open.

At this moment they heard the sounds—the screeches and howls of angry animals. Peering out across the distant flats, they could make out the black horde approaching. Hundreds of hungry beasts were rushing toward them. "Quick! Everyone inside!" Tropas yelled.

"They finally got here," said Moss. "Well, we were expectin' them."

"Don't panic, but be quick," ordered Tropas. He stood aside as the crowd pressed on into the station. Tropas was the last to duck inside, just as the first beasts leaped up the embankment. He shoved the heavy door shut, and Rocco slammed down the lock bar. They could hear the creatures outside yelping, pounding, scratching on the door.

"We're safe in here," said Rocco. "There is no way they can get into this station."

"And no way we can get out," lamented Moss.

27

The interior of the AG station was anything but comfortable—dark walls and ceiling, damp, stuffy atmosphere, with little ventilation. It was not designed to accommodate crowds of people. It was assumed that the technicians who came to activate the device would not need to linger here long. Low benches were placed around the walls, but not enough seating for 40 people. Most were forced to stand in place. Lighting was adequate, but there was little of interest to look upon.

The people had brought no food or water with them. Worst of all, there were no toilet facilities. If they were forced to stay here longer than an hour or so, this place would become intolerable. But they dare not open the door. The Kestler beasts were waiting outside, beating and clawing on the steel. They knew there was food inside. They were not going away soon.

Tropas knew he had to hurry. It was already becoming hard to breathe. He stood before the massive console in the middle of the station. He stared at the rows of dials and switches. Could he make sense of these? "Rocco, can you give me any help here? Can you tell me anything about this system?"

"I know you switch on the main power by turning the knurled wheel there at the top. After that, you know as much about this damned machine as I do." Tropas turned the wheel. The device began to hum, and a white button on the top left of the console lit up. "Oh yeah, I remember something else. Yipper told me the little mnemonic trick that gets you started—'Push the white, move left to right.' That was it. Make any sense to you?"

"It might. Let me think a minute."

"Not much of a clue, buddy. Just seven little words."

"But it's a start," said Tropas. "It's a way to start." *Push the white. That has to mean press the white button that's glowing.* He pushed it, and the first row of dials lighted. *Eureka! Dials, I can handle. I wasn't a weatherman for nothing. Move left to right. Start with the dial on the far left. But first I have to push the rocker switch under the dial.* He turned the dial knob, and the needle swung across the white face. When it reached the green, a small orange light appeared over the second dial. *Hit the rocker switch, turn the knob, and let the needle swing over to the green. Next dial gets the orange light, telling me it's ready to go. Rocker, knob, green, and so on and so on, from left to right. I can do this! I know how to switch on the AG device! But I have to go through five rows of dials.*

While Tropas worked, the people handled the pressure as best they could. The ark had tilted farther. Now everyone could feel it. ***Proteus*** was slowly slipping toward this new world. The ark was being dragged farther into its field. Soon the craft would begin to accelerate toward the surface.

Dr. Brownlee sat and wrote in his journal. He was composing what he believed would be his final entry.

They are outside the door, beating, howling, slavering. We can hear them clawing at the steel. They want our flesh. Hundreds of black fiends. They are animals, creatures without souls, driven by their insatiable hunger. I find it almost impossible to believe they were once rational human beings.

I think we may soon be the only survivors—perhaps three dozen men, women, and children. Our sanctuary is the anti-grav station in the aft portion of the ark. We fled here and sealed the heavy door, but now we find ourselves confined to this metal tomb from which there is no escape. We are safe for now, but we have no food, no water. Breathing is already becoming difficult. There are too many of us. Within a few hours we will all suffocate.

As I pen what will, no doubt, be my final entry, I can see young Tropas standing before a bank of dials feverishly manipulating the controls. He is a brave lad. He will not give up. But

I fear it is useless. We are already beginning to fall. Our proud vessel will plunge onto the surface of this unknown planet and we will all perish. Our destiny has almost run its course. Farewell.

As soon as Tropas completed the final row of dials, a green light flashed at the top of the console and the machine began emitting a series of sharp tones. These continued for a minute before shutting down. The green light glowed above the banks of dials, indicating that the device was functioning.

"Yipper said that when the device turned on, it would sing for a minute and there'd be a steady green light at the top. So you must have figured it out, Tropas. Congratulations! You're one smart trooper."

"What happens now?" asked Moss.

"We wait," answered Rocco, "and we brace for the impact. Right now we're falling. We can't feel it, but we're going down fast, just not as fast as we would have."

Tropas went and knelt beside Gabriella. "We've done all we can, Mom. We have to hope for the best now. I think we'll come through this okay. I have faith and so should you. You and Marla hold onto something real tight. You'll feel a big jolt soon."

28

The fall of the ark produced a tumult beyond imagination. The ***Proteus*** descended onto a mountain range in what would be considered the northern hemisphere of Centris-C. The impact could be heard a hundred miles away—had there been human ears to detect it. The resultant earthquake shook the trees in distant valleys. The ark's shattered hull lay across twin snow-covered peaks. The craft was devastated but not annihilated, demolished but not destroyed. Its outer shell was twisted, warped, and fractured. The ark would never rise again. Its bones would rest on these mountaintops for countless eons.

The anti-gravity device had greatly reduced the ark's velocity upon impact. However, the feature that prevented more massive destruction was the ocean of water carried in its bow. This served as an effective cushion softening the impact when the ark dived in bow first. Millions of gallons of water exploded outward and cascaded down the mountainsides in a tremendous tsunami, forming into pools and lakes in the green valley below.

Inside the ***Proteus***, the devastation was truly profound. The twin cylinders, Alpha and Omega, which had rotated continuously for two millennia, stopped their turning when they were crushed together upon impact. Then when the body of the ark rumbled over onto its side, the planet's gravity played havoc with all things lining the cylinders' inner surfaces. Millions of tons of soil lying on the upper faces came crashing down, as well as trees, houses, and black fiends—a massive deluge that rained down six miles to form a thick blanket of utter ruination below.

Tropas and his people were miraculously sheltered inside the anti-grav station. They were bounced and bruised. There were concussions and two broken bones. But they all survived. None died. They waited hours in the dark after the chaos subsided. When they finally dared open the door, they found the black fiends had vanished. The AG station had landed fairly upright, although the people were forced to struggle down a steep incline before reaching level ground. In the distance they could see daylight through a gash in the ark's outer shell. But this was miles away, more than a day's journey. Tropas realized they must leave the ark. They must walk out under the sun. They had no choice. The ***Proteus***, which had been their home, now was their death trap. They could not defend themselves in the darkness. They would be easy prey for any surviving black fiends that chanced upon them. The greatest hazard they faced, however, was invisible. Tropas knew that the four nuclear reactors, as well as the SAC, had probably ruptured in the crash. Even now, they might be swimming in lethal radiation. They dared not take a chance; they must leave the ark as soon as possible and then distance themselves from it.

Tropas led them toward the light. They must move on, despite pain and hunger. They had no supplies, no food or water. But they were alive. They would survive. They could perhaps find enough edible roots, berries, and grains to stave off starvation—even in the darkness. One does what one must. And so they began the brutal trek toward the sunlight.

Tropas stood on a pinnacle of rock and gazed off into the valley far below. He knew they would travel there soon. Snow blanketed the ground all around. Flakes drifted down in the morning sunlight. Behind him his friends huddled together in the shadow of the fallen ark. Someone had kindled a small fire, and several were gathered around its warmth.

A hundred yards distant, black fiends were clambering out of a second rupture in the ship's hull. But they posed no threat. They scampered off down the mountainside and disappeared. *They hate the cold*, he said to himself. *They seek warmer habitats down below.*

There was much to do. He and a few of the men might

risk a brief expedition back into the ark to scavenge supplies before abandoning it forever. Soon they must seek out a more hospitable locale. They must travel into the green valley to establish themselves, to find fish and game. They must explore this new world which was to become their home. They must learn all they could—and quickly. Today they were strangers in this strange new land, but that would change. He, Tropas Bojeon, would lead them and teach them if they would allow him to. This small band of cold, ragged human beings was poised on the edge. He would help them meet impossible challenges, grow together, and begin a new life.

Roselyn came to him and took his hand. "Come to the fire, Tropas. I think you're too cold standing here. You will be ill."

"In a minute, dear girl. My head is full of plans and dreams. I need to ponder them awhile."

He inhaled deeply. He liked this land. The air was rich and fresh. It invigorated him. And the rock he stood on was solid and secure. Yes, they would prosper here in this new world. They would discover new happiness.

The drifting flakes caressed his face and hair. He smiled, and his heart was at peace.

FROM THE AUTHOR

This novel, *Fall of the Ark*, is a prequel to an earlier work, *Kestler's Bane* (Outskirts Press, 2017). This current book presents a kind of back story for the saga of Truman Hale, Marlianna, and the "Boat People," whose ancestors "fell from the sky." If you've completed *Fall of the Ark*, but have not yet read *Kestler's Bane*, then I urge you to do so. I think you will appreciate how the tales are linked together. If you have read *Kestler's Bane*, but have not yet begun *Fall of the Ark*, then why are you now reading this last page, you silly goose? Why aren't you on page one, beginning this marvelous story?

I feel an obligation to remind you, Dear Reader, that we all live in perilous times. Please be careful to avoid the Queen from the East, who, like Kestler's dark fiends, spreads disease and misery in her wake. Be circumspect, and stay safe!

Happy reading always,
Jago Muir
April, 2021

ABOUT THE AUTHOR

Jago Muir is a graduate of the University of North Texas, where he took a B.A. in English in the 1960s. He later did Master's work at Lamar University in Beaumont, Texas. His study of linguistics and the English language earned him a place as a scholarly writer, publishing his work in the *Lamar Journal of the Humanities*.

Muir is a lover of diversity with an extremely low threshold for boredom. He is a teacher, poet, musical composer, and singer. When he takes a break from writing, he enjoys playing folk guitar and bluegrass banjo, and regularly performing karaoke. He is also a private pilot, an amateur magician, a belted martial artist, a chess aficionado, and a fluent speaker of French and Mandarin.

Muir currently lives in Liuzhou, China, where he teaches English as a foreign language. His wife, Xue Qing Wen, teaches philosophy and English at Laibin Vocational College.

Also by JAGO MUIR

Meet The Boys From

Crud Hall

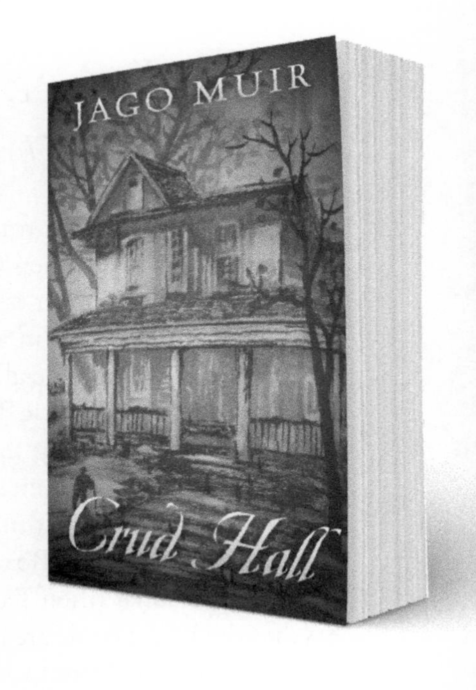

Follow the adventures of Harvey Smith and his hell-raising college buddies from Crud Hall, an off-campus rooming house at a major university. The early 1960s was a defining period in American history—the Civil Rights Movement was underway, the urban folk music revival was mushrooming on college campuses, and a place called Vietnam was getting national attention. The Crud Hall stories reflect the mores, mind set, and values of many American university students during this era. Meet Harvey and his friends—Crunch, Bear, Weed, and all the rest of the screwball gang. Hilarious, raunchy, irreverent, the Crud Hall boys will touch your heart and mind in a very special way.

"I laughed until I hurt. Jago Muir has a wicked sense of humor. His tongue-in-cheek descriptions will hit you full in the face, while his subtleties will sometimes slip right by you if you blink."

—Terry Richard, former editor for Lamar University Press

"A hillbilly who pimps for his wife? A neon Oriental pagoda on the roof of a Mexican brothel? A bodybuilder afraid of rabbits? Where does Muir come up with these wonderful, weird ideas?

—Beth Parker, MEd, MS

Also by
JAGO MUIR

Kestler's Bane
The Proteus Chronicles

The year is 5465 C.E. A routine mission goes horribly wrong when Captain Truman Hale's space cruiser is destroyed in a freak storm. He lands in an unfamiliar world, where five strange allies join him. Together they must battle The Molester, the leader of horrifying creatures who live in an underground maze, torturing and devouring their victims...especially the peaceful and gentle Boat People. The war turns personal when Truman discovers that the Boat People are his own kind: humans descended from survivors of the Proteus, a space ark launched from Earth in the 22nd century. In the ultimate test of bravery and loyalty, the six warriors must unite against the forces of darkness, while unraveling the hidden secrets sheltered in this unique world. This gripping saga will linger in your imagination long after you have turned the final page.

Learn more at:
www.outskirtspress.com/kestlersbane

Also by JAGO MUIR

Libido

Rise of the Ox

You'll howl as Harvey encounters a Cajun "grabber" and a porpoising Cessna Cardinal. But then things turn dark when he finds himself caught up in an FBI investigation of a double murder. What is the mysterious Ox Club? Who are its members, and what baleful, unholy rituals do they practice? Finally, what is the terrible secret carried by Maybelle Lowther, Harvey's mentally challenged sophomore student? You'll find yourself shocked, but mesmerized, as this gripping story continues.

Learn more at:
www.outskirtspress.com/libidoriseoftheox

Also by
JAGO MUIR

Libido
The Shattering

The accidental death of two popular students devastates Glenby High School. Indeed, the entire community is shattered. And soon afterwards the town must cope with the tragedy of Maybelle Lowther, this coming right before Christmas and followed quickly by a ghastly discovery—the tortured remains of her father, a prominent businessman, high-ranking Freemason, and deacon in the First Baptist Church. What satanic forces have been let loose in this small Texas town, and how is the mysterious Ox Club involved? The answers perhaps lie hidden in a secret cache of 8mm home movie reels discovered in the Lowther mansion. The shocking resolution of this grotesque story is steeped in pure evil. Read it and be afraid.

Also by
JAGO MUIR

The Death Wall

And other early stories and poems

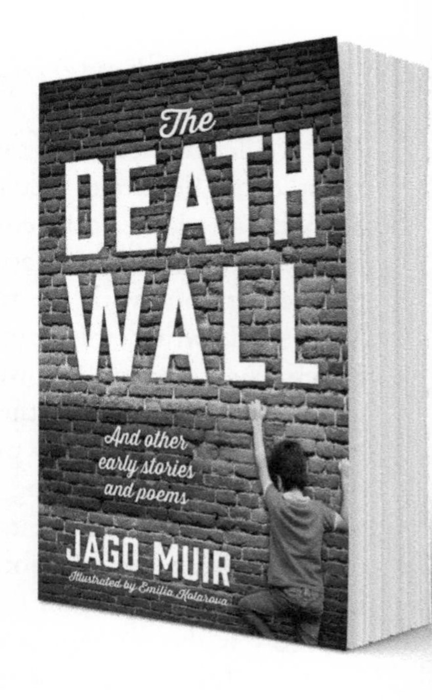

Hidden for 40 years, they are found in a box of old books! The accidental discovery of a cache of manuscripts—stories and poems he wrote long ago—leads the author on a journey through time. Here is an eclectic mixture, including a bizarre nursery rhyme, a "troggy" jump rope chant, a magic junk house, zombie forest musicians, and a little boy who wants to climb the "death wall." Travel back with Muir to the 1960s as he provides intimate glimpses into his early life, his views as a young man on love, brotherhood, and the Christian faith. This diverse mixture of delightful prose and poetry will make you laugh and weep . . .and think.

Also by
JAGO MUIR

Glenby Harvest

Taking his cue from James Joyce's Dubliners, Jago Muir offers up twelve stories about people from his hometown, Glenby, Texas. An eclectic mixture, we are given touches of humor and mystery—a sloppy airplane landing, a midnight trip down a lonely dirt road seeking a ghost light. But we also find twisted sketches of men and women consumed by moral depravity, given to incestuous lust, sadistic abuse, even murder most foul. Meet these Glenby travelers and journey down this road with them. It's an experience you won't soon forget.

Learn more at:
www.outskirtspress.com/aglenbyharvest

Lightning Source UK Ltd.
Milton Keynes UK
UKHW041351060821
388423UK00001BA/78